Sea Serpent

A JTF-13 Legacy Novel

By:

John S. Worth

Three Ravens Publishing
Chickamauga, GA

Dedication, Acknowledgements, and Thanks

Dedication

This novel is dedicated to the men and women who paid the ultimate price in service to their nation - the Sailors, Marines, Soldiers, and Airmen of the United States Armed Forces and their families. Though the monsters depicted in these pages are fictional, all who have served know there are very real threats which must be opposed, often at a very high cost.

I dedicate this especially to the crews of the *USS Stark* and *USS Cole*. The tragic events which befell these brave men and women are sobering reminders of the evil that exists in the world. Their sacrifice in the line of duty and the determination of those who survived serve as examples of the love which will ultimately conquer that evil. I hope that this story, though fictional, might in some small way pay homage to your memory and further ensure we never forget.

Acknowledgements

I want to give a shout out to the crew of the *USS Hayler*, with whom I had the privilege to serve. You guys were the best. A few of you may see hints of yourselves in some of the characters depicted here. There might also be some scenes based on true events, though I've purposely altered the order to suit the needs of the story.

From the search and rescue we performed following the tragic explosion of Piper Alpha to the dozens of ports explored, each experience shaped me as I transitioned into manhood. It wasn't always pretty, but it was as real as it gets. So another shout out to the United States Navy itself, for showing me the world and giving me such a fine band of brothers along the way. I am forever grateful.

Thanks

I want to thank John F. Holmes. Without his open call for submissions in the shared universe of JTF13, it's very likely I never would have written this book. This story stretched me as a writer and took me down memory lane, while also allowing my imagination to run wild.

I am also extremely grateful to Scott Tackett and Three Ravens Publishing for taking the reins when it looked like the JTF13 project would either fall to the wayside or its various titles be left to the authors to publish and push individually. I very much appreciate you pulling us authors in, breathing new life into JTF13, and giving us a proper relaunch. Your willingness to reach out and take on such an endeavor is generous beyond belief and simply amazing! Also, your editorial suggestions and corrections made my novel so much stronger than it would have otherwise been (Any remaining mistakes are completely on me). I'm convinced I'm a better writer as a result. So, thanks again!

I also want to thank the members of the following Facebook groups: Cannon Publishing Writer's Group, the Command Post, the Squirrel's Nest, and JTF13 Working Group. Thanks to all of you for the ongoing encouragement. I'm glad I found you.

Many, many thanks to my patient, loving wife, Staci Elizabeth. I'm so grateful for all the hours you allowed me to work on this endeavor. It means the world to me to have you in my corner. I truly couldn't do it without you, and I love you with all my heart.

To my sons, Caleb and Levi, thanks for all the feedback on the sea serpent I designed. You're both gifted artists and have eyes for design that are far beyond your years. The cover is stronger because of you both.

Finally, to my Lord and Savior, Jesus Christ. I feel your pleasure and the presence of your Holy Spirit when I write or create art of any kind. Though this story is not overly focused on the spiritual aspects of my Christian faith, there is an unseen world that often impacts this physical realm. That theme is woven into these pages as well as those of sacrifice, friendship, and love. I pray those timeless and universal truths will shine through my often dark and treacherous tale. Thank you, Lord, for co-laboring with me.

Peace,
John S. Worth
2021

Two terrible, defining moments marked his Naval career: May 17, 1987, when Iraqi missiles struck the *USS Stark*, and October 12, 2000, when Al-Qaeda attacked the *USS Cole*. The events were separated by roughly thirteen years. Whether coincidental or not, this seemed in hindsight a grim confirmation of Thomas McCraith's calling.

This is his story…

Part One: Recruit

John S. Worth

Chapter 1

May 17, 1987
Coronado, California
1130 hours

Seaman Thomas "Red" McCraith doubled over from the sudden, sharp pain—right in the pit of his gut. His stomach lurched and his heart fluttered like a bird caught in his ribcage. "What the hell?" he muttered. He started breathing slowly, calming himself. He looked around to ensure no one else had seen.

He put a hand on a nearby post and steadied himself. He started walking again toward the barracks. This was the end of week one of phase three BUD/S—Basic Underwater Demolition/SEAL—training, no way he'd let an onset of nerves derail him now. Sure, he'd had his doubts. Everyone did. That was normal though, wasn't it?

Once inside his barracks, he caught wind of the scuttlebutt, which quickly became an onslaught of rumor and speculation. With the grim rasp of death, the news had everyone astir. He hurried back outside. Found the nearest phone and made a collect call.

Though he tried to hide emotion, his trembling voice betrayed him, "Is it true?"

"Just saw it on the news, son." His father's tone seemed uncertain as if wanting to reassure—but, as always, unwilling to sugar-coat. "Nobody knows much right now, but ... yeah, something's happened."

Red felt himself beginning to falter. "I should've been there. We signed up on the buddy system, then I abandoned him."

His father's voice grew firm, "Listen Tom, we don't know anything yet. So don't jump to conclusions. You took an opportunity. Hell, if you'd been there, *you* might be dead."

"I should have stayed on the *Stark*."

"Calm down, Tommy. Take a minute and just—"

"He's dead. I feel it in my gut." Red hung up on his father, then he marched straight out and across the yard.

Within moments he'd reached the bell. Red put a hand on the cord and swallowed hard. Ran his free hand slowly across his brow, trying not to break down.

The weight of what he was doing flashed in his mind; *DOR, drop on request. No turning back if you do this.* Whether it was his father's voice or just his own troubled thoughts, Red couldn't tell. He finally decided it didn't matter.

He rang the bell.

On the other side of the world, in the depths of the Red Sea, a malevolent presence stirred. Though roughly a thousand miles from the recent conflict, the ancient demi-god, Saxüru, felt the veil between worlds fracture, like a fissure running across ancient lands and seas.

He approached the dimensional rift and slipped through. After years of containment, he once more crossed over into the world of men.

Rising from the trenches, he surveyed the underwater terrain with pale, golden eyes. He sensed the aftermath of violent destruction. Death on the waters again. War raged on among the offspring of those who once worshipped him in Babylon. And finally, it had spilled into the brine.

Saxüru grinned, his teeth like sharp, curved chisels. His nostrils flared, pulling deep breaths of water while taking in the scents. He reared his head, thrusting back with his thick, curled horns. He stroked along the currents with arms adorned in patches of tangled fur and iridescent scales. Each hand had two jointed fingers with one short, opposable stub. Thick and dark, the digits were like long, cloven hooves. He gave a flick of his fish-like tail and sped through the water.

He soon found a jutting rock above the seabed and atop an underwater ridge. Saxüru struck the stone with his hooves and horns until a rudimentary throne was hewn into its surface. He curled his broad, scalloped tail beneath him, draped his arms across the rests on each side, and began to survey his kingdom. Then, chattering loudly in an all but forgotten tongue, he called to the creatures of the deep, announcing his arrival.

"Your Master has returned," he proclaimed. *"Tell all your kindred; the Ancient One, Saxüru, now reigns."*

About a week after his arrival, Saxüru ventured to the surface, his destination the shore. The being had been called by many names: Saxüru, Saxuibex, Capricorn, and a host of others. He was of the Annunaki, once revered as gods and then consigned to legend. Separated from the realm of men when doorways were closed and barriers between worlds shut up tight.

Though the region of the human world adjacent to that of his home had always been restless and plagued with war, the wall between dimensions had held firm for many years. Until now.

These were Saxüru's musings as he entered the shallows and began his metamorphosis. His tail split lengthwise, forming two jointed legs. His face shortened, shrinking in to form the flattened, yet indistinct visage of a human. The major digits of each hoof parted, as each set of two fingers transformed into four. Finally, his horns slowly retracted into his skull.

He strode up onto the land of a lush bay, where a wandering Bedouin watched awestruck while this feral being marched naked from the sea. Without warning, Saxüru rushed the man, grabbed him by the forehead with one hand while striking hard, crushing the windpipe with the other. Within moments the man sprawled dead upon the ground.

Saxüru divested the corpse of a huge pouch made of oiled camel hide. Finely stitched and entirely watertight, it hung from one shoulder by a sturdy leather strap. Saxüru dumped its contents on the ground, dates, bread, and other foods. Then he took the man's clothing and wrapped himself in the undergarments and robes.

He removed the leggings and boots as well, putting them in the pouch for later. From the man's dead fingers, he pried a long walking staff of gnarled wood; its surface was mottled gray and white, polished to a faint sheen. He walked on, barefoot upon the sand, his features still changing as he took on the countenance of the man.

This would now be his permanent visage while in human form. The face of the first man he killed since returning to this plane. Though powerful, there were limitations to his abilities, even in this realm. Saxüru did not question it. It had always been so. Besides, he had a plan to put in motion; a purpose to fulfill.

A new season of unrest was simmering to a boil. Conflict led to conflict, like brush fires slowly spreading, momentarily quelled only to break out again. Dissent was steadily building, war ever threatening to erupt. Weapons were once again creating fissures and rifts through which Saxüru could pass and lead his subjects through.

More than that, things long in slumber were awakening, heralding the dawn of a new era. Perhaps it was time to dwell once again beside mankind, to once more rule and bask in the power of life-force released in bloody warfare and ritual sacrifice.

To once more reign as a God.

Chapter 2

Over one year later: July 06, 1988
Scotland, on the streets of Edinburgh
1800 hours

Wanting to celebrate his recent promotion to E-4, Petty Officer Third Class 'Red' McCraith and a few other Deck Dawgs, including Seaman Mateo Ortiz and Seaman Dale 'Smitty' Smith, wasted no time when the workday ended. Their duty team was finally off and there was a city out there to explore. Inside an hour they were walking south from Ferry Road to hit one of the oldest pubs in Edinburgh.

Still, the two seamen were openly impatient with their friend's morbid detour.

Ortiz asked, "What's wrong with him, Smitty? Is this one of those 'Southern things' I wouldn't understand?"

"Hell no," said Smitty, shaking his head. "I can tell you right now, ain't nothing Southern about wanting to go strolling through no graveyard."

"Well, least it's not dark yet," said Ortiz. "You hear that Red? Better get your jollies now, 'cause we're not coming back once that sun is down. Don't care if you got frocked BM3, Bosun with a crow on his sleeve. Ain't taking no unlawful or ungodly orders to go pokin' around in a cemetery after dark."

"Y'all really are a couple of morons." Red slowed down and turned to face them. "My last name is McCraith. Put two and two together."

Smith got a confused look on his face. "Four? Okay, you got me, Red. What the hell does 'four' got to do with anything?"

Ortiz slapped the back of Smith's head. "It's his last name, Smitty. Damn. This is Scotland and all. His homeland. Reason for that head full of ugly-ass orange hair."

"Least I ain't no banana eatin' Puerto Rican."

Smitty laughed and Ortiz bowed up. "Don't make me put you in the sleeper hold. You know I was State champ in High School."

"First, Puerto Rico is not a state," Red pointed out, "And second, we'll roll out that mat anytime you get ready."

Ortiz laughed. "I got him scared, Smitty. You see how he backpedaled there."

Smith had that lost look on his face again.

Red just smiled as they pulled in step beside him.

"It's because he made Third Class so quick," Ortiz went on. "He's all 'I got my first chevron, I'm a genius. Gotta trace my genealogy to see if I come from a line of geniuses.' That's what this is about, huh Red?"

"I'm looking for my great grandfather's grave. I told Grandpa I would find it if I could and take a picture, then see if there's any others around that might be of interest. He's into that stuff. It's really kinda cool."

"Sorry, man." Ortiz shook his head decidedly. "Nothing cool about hanging out in a graveyard. Day or night. We just coming along so somebody's got your back. Can't let a bunch of Royal Navy pukes jump you in some back alley and beat you down for being American and all."

"Do they do that?" asked Smitty.

"Not with us around they won't," said Ortiz.

"Yeah," Red agreed, "Ortiz'll put 'em in the sleeper hold. Two at a time."

Ortiz stuck out his chest. "Damn straight."

Red stopped and pointed ahead. "There it is."

About two blocks down, on the other side of an intersection, was Rosebank Cemetery. They walked in silence for the next few blocks and crossed over the intersection onto Pilrig Street. The entire cemetery was surrounded by a stone wall, with an opening right ahead.

The place was filled with obelisks, Celtic crosses, marble and granite slabs. Though many looked timeworn, none were truly ancient.

"This graveyard was started in the 1840's," Red told them. "My great grandpa was a member of the Royal

Scots and died fighting in World War One. He's somewhere in here."

At that, the two other men grew solemn and respectful. In a whisper, Smitty asked, "How you wanna do this, Red? Want us to spread out or something?"

Red shook his head. "I've got a general idea where to look. Y'all just stick with me. And you ain't got to whisper. Not like we're gonna wake 'em up or something." He led them through the cemetery, pausing now and then to read a headstone, but moving steadily toward the far corner.

"Your grandpa all the way in the back?" Ortiz asked.

"Close to the back, I think," Red answered.

Ortiz glanced about nervously. "Of course, he is. All the way in the back. That sun is getting low, brother." An errant blade of tall grass brushed his arm and he jerked away, stumbling into Red.

Red laughed. "There's nothing to be afraid of. We're in a city with lots of people. Look..." He pointed beyond the far wall of the cemetery. "Those are apartment buildings. Everywhere there's buildings. We're gonna be fine."

"Right. Let's just get on with it, okay."

When they got to the far corner, Red pointed to a monument. "You guys see that?"

A large memorial marked a mass grave, with the stone wall directly behind it. Red led them to the memorial. It was a large Celtic cross, with a roaring lion carved halfway up the column. Beneath the lion were the words, "To those who gave their lives for their country".

Red pointed at the bottom plaque and read it aloud. "In memory of officers, non-commissioned officers, and men... who met their death at Gretna on 22nd May 1915, in a terrible railway disaster on their way to fight for their country."

Ortiz read the verse at the end, "Yea, though I walk through the valley of the shadow of death, I will fear no evil: for Thou art with me." He closed his eyes and genuflected.

Red stepped back and pulled a camera from his pocket. He snapped a photo, advanced the film, and took another for good measure.

"That's some harsh fate right there," said Ortiz. "All ready to throw down and then get killed in some freak accident. So was your great grandpa with them?"

"No," Red admitted, "But look at all those names." On either side of the large cross, against the cemetery's back wall, stood two wide, ornate stone monuments. Each monument bore five large plagues, mounted side by side. All bearing the names of the dead. "Two hundred and fifteen soldiers."

"That's about as many sailors on our ship," said Smitty.

"Damn," said Ortiz. "Kind of makes you think, doesn't it? I mean, we're not at war, but things can go sideways pretty fast and next thing you know..." He made a slight shrug as he raised his eyebrows.

Red paused. "We're probably closer than you guys think."

"What do you mean?" asked Smitty.

Red spelled things out again. "About a year ago. Matter of fact it was last May, the *USS Stark*, remember?"

Ortiz snapped his fingers. "Yeah, I remember that. Over thirty sailors killed. Whose jet was it fired those missiles? Iran or Iraq?"

"It was Iraq," Red informed him. "But I blame both of 'em since they're at war with each other and we got caught in the crossfire. I tell you guys, that Persian Gulf is a powder keg." He shook his head. "Thirty-seven sailors."

"Where is the Persian Gulf?" asked Smitty.

Red closed his eyes and turned away. "Let's find this grave and get to the pub already."

Within minutes he'd located the headstone. It was small and nondescript. With the name Malcolm McCraith carved into a marble slab and the dates 1888 - 1916 carved beneath. "Only a year after grandpa was born," Red whispered. He took two photos, then handed the camera to Ortiz. "Take a picture of me next to it."

"Sure thing." Ortiz took the camera as Red knelt beside the stone. Once he was ready, one arm around the short headstone and the other hanging off his knee, he looked up at Ortiz. "That's right, don't smile. This is a serious moment," said Ortiz. "You ready?"

Red gave a slight nod.

Ortiz snapped the picture, advanced the film. "One more." He took another, advanced the film again, and handed it back. "We ready now?"

Red put the camera away, then held up a finger. "One more thing." He reached into another pocket and pulled out a folded sheet of tracing paper. Then he fished a grease pencil from his shirt pocket.

"Where'd you get those?" asked Smitty.

Red unfolded the paper and pressed it flat against the stone, creased it over the top so it wouldn't fall off. He had way more than enough. "I got this paper from Vincent down in CIC. And there's grease pencils everywhere, so who knows."

"That's that paper they use on that DRT thing, ain't it?" Smitty asked.

"What does that even stand for?" asked Ortiz.

"Dead Reckoning Trace." Red pushed a thumbnail into the black wrapping of the grease pencil. He pulled at it, unraveling a narrow, tan strip to expose a long section of the black core. Then he broke that piece away and put the pencil back in his pocket.

John S. Worth

"Dead Reckoning?" said Ortiz. "Man, all they do is draw lines on it and little symbols for the ship. Why they gotta make it sound all techy? Like it's some super high level—"

"It's just a way to keep track of where we've been and what was around us at the time." Red proceeded to make a rubbing of the headstone. Like magic, the words and dates appeared in a stark contrast, as well as details not readily visible. Designs of thistles, vines, and a Celtic-knot cross, all etched into the stone. "Grandpa's gonna love this," he said as he finished the rubbing.

Just then the air was rent by a mournful scream. Red dropped the paper, startled. He stumbled to his feet. "What the hell?"

It came from the corner of the graveyard, where they'd stood before. A white-haired woman faced the monument, her back to him. She was draped in gray swaths that hung from her thin limbs like Spanish moss from an oak. She turned to face him.

Red's pulse quickened and his mouth went dry. A chill sank its teeth into the evening air, instantly dropping the temperature. He took a single step back while his stomach seemed to crawl, squirming deeper toward his bowels. The evening chill sent a tendril of ice snaking down his spine.

Her face was pale and bright as a full moon, her eyes like pools of blood. She opened her mouth and shrieked again.

Red shoved his hands to his ears, trying to maintain composure and control of his bowels. "Whoa, what's wrong with her?" He turned to his friends. "Hey guys..."

They were gone.

Red squinted toward the direction of the entrance. He thought he saw one of them dart past an obelisk. Then they were out.

He bent to pick up the paper. "Sure am glad y'all got my back. Wouldn't want any Royal Navy pukes to—" Before his hand could close on the paper it was snatched away.

Red straightened, ready to chase a windblown page. Instead, he found himself face to face with the woman, so close he could see the blue veins beneath her pallid skin. She was opening her mouth for another scream.

He took another quick step back and pulled the camera from his pocket. Before him stood the woman, skeletal yet stately. He noticed her feet did not touch the ground. In one hand she held the rubbing he'd made. She screamed a third time.

Red held up the camera and struck the picture. Advanced the film and hastily took another. It was his last. The film would advance no further. He shoved the camera back in his pocket, looked at the woman, and pointed. "Sorry, but can't leave without that." He rushed forward to snatch the paper from her hand.

As he pulled it, she let it go, but with the fingers of her free hand she touched the back of his neck. Red found himself flying through the air, but still holding onto the paper. He landed on a grassy patch of earth, rolled, and found himself staring up at the cemetery's back wall.

Quickly he got his feet under him again. He folded the paper to put it away, as he looked around, but saw no trace of the woman. "Hey! Hello! Crypt-keeper screaming woman!"

No answer. Red looked at the nearest wall. He could probably scale it. But then he saw the verse on the bottom of the cross and said, "I will fear no evil." He turned back the way he'd come. Determined not to run, he made a deliberate effort to calm his nerves as he walked toward the entrance. He made it back to Pilrig Street without incident.

Red caught up with his shipmates at the Tolbooth Tavern, an old historic pub. They were already sitting with pints in front of them.

He walked to the bar. "Two fingers of The Glenlivet 21 year. Neat."

The bartender eyed him quizzically. He pushed a pair of round spectacles up on his wide face. "A Yank who knows his whisky! I'm impressed."

"Well, I *am* American," Red agreed, "But where I'm from we don't exactly call ourselves 'Yank'. Reb would be more acceptable."

The bartender poured the scotch and grinned. "Oh, yer a southern man then."

Red pulled out his wallet to pay. "From Georgia. Last name's McCraith, but my friends call me Red. What do I owe you?"

"McCraith? Have ye come home then, lad?" The bartender set the bottle down.

"My great grandpa is buried up at Rosebank cemetery. So, in a way, I reckon so."

The man pushed the tumbler closer to Red. "First one's on the house then. Try not to fall in love with the land of yer forefathers. You may never want to leave."

"Much obliged." Red's hand curled around the drink. "And it might be too late already. Now excuse me while I chastise a couple of pansies." He raised the glass to the barkeep.

The man flicked a lazy salute, dragging fingertips by his temple.

Red took a seat and let them have it. "Thought you knuckle-draggers had my back."

Ortiz had his pint to his face. Smitty sat his down and said, "Sorry Red, but when it comes to a haint, it's every man for himself."

Ortiz gulped and added, "She was *not* human. And besides, I got an eardrum was punctured in childhood. Last thing I need is to go out on some lame-ass medical discharge."

The bartender hastily made his way over. "Sorry, but did I hear that right? Were ye sayin' somethin' about a haint?"

Ortiz nodded. "Out by the graveyard. She was floating, dressed in a rotted gown."

Smitty nodded. "And she was screaming louder than a —"

"A baen-sith," said the bartender.

Smitty shook his head. "No, it was an old woman with red eyes. She was crying and wailing."

"Screaming," said Ortiz.

"Okay. Ye might be more familiar with the term *banshee*," the barkeep said.

"As in screaming like a banshee?" asked Red.

"Aye. The keening woman of the fairy folk. A harbinger of death."

Red's skin pricked as he remembered her touch. "So, what do we need to do?"

The man pushed his spectacles up his nose. "Pray she weren't keening fer you."

"I'm sorry," said Ortiz. "Language barriers and all that. What exactly does *keening* mean?"

"Ah, it's a song of lament, for the dead. A most sorrowful sound."

"Yeah," Red agreed. "That it was."

"If it *were* a baen-sith, be on yer guards, lads." The bartender wandered back to his post. For the next several minutes none of them said a word, just kept at their drinks.

Finally, Ortiz broke the silence. "Glad we got out of there. She might have killed us."

"Dead as a doornail," Smitty agreed. "Hey, where do y'all reckon that saying comes from?"

Ortiz and Red both shook their heads.

They went on like that for almost an hour, then Red noticed their chief walk in. He drew their attention to the big Boatswain's Mate. "Looks like Chief Ingram's flying solo."

"Man, I hope he doesn't see us," said Ortiz. "I get tired of that old salt riding my back."

Smitty shrugged. "Maybe he'll buy us a round."

His friends stared in bewilderment. "Smitty, I love you, bro..." Red clasped him by a shoulder. "But of all the stupid things you could say—"

"That was the stupidest!" Ortiz finished for him.

John S. Worth

Before Smitty could reply, their Chief pulled out a bosun's whistle and blew a shrill note.

"Damn thing's worse than that banshee," Ortiz said, covering his ears.

"Everybody pipe down and listen up!" Chief Ingram stood at the bar of the old pub. All eyes went to him and the noise in the small establishment dropped to a murmur.

Red got a sinking feeling in his stomach.

"For all crewmembers of the *USS Hayler*, this shore-leave just ended. We've got a distress call in the North Sea and all hands are to prepare to get underway. Don't get left behind gentlemen! We've got paddy wagons working with us around the clock to haul you boys in. Get your asses to Ferry Road and they'll drive you in from there."

Red sighed and downed his Scotch. They stood, along with the other sailors in the room, mostly enlisted, but also a few officers.

As they ambled past Ingram, Smitty told Red, "Hope we ain't walking back by that cemetery."

"We definitely are not," said Ortiz.

Once they were outside, Red whispered, "Fellas, we might wanna keep quiet about all that. Don't think we want any shrinks asking a bunch of questions and giving us psych exams."

"Yeah," said Ortiz, "Either that or a piss test." He laughed. "Or both."

"Hell, at least we can *pass* a piss test," said Smitty.

At that they all laughed.

John S. Worth

Chapter 3

July 07, 1988
Destroyer *USS Hayler*, DD-997
The North Sea, in transit to *Piper Alpha* oil platform

It had been one crazy night. Most of the crew were aboard when the distress call came through, but the night had been relatively young and about eighty sailors were ashore. There was a dedicated effort to bring everyone in. Even if they were half-hammered. By 0100 all hands were accounted for as the crew mustered on the helo deck for their briefing.

By 0200, stations were manned, and the ship got underway. Red relieved the port lookout at 0350. It was miles of dark ocean for another hour. Then the sky began to brighten, and just like a tree full of birds, the young men on the JL circuit started chirping away, both to wake themselves and pass the time while they waited for the unknown.

At 0620 the sun was finally up. Stationed at port lookout, Red squinted toward the horizon. The sun was finally up, and it was going to be a long day. In the dim light of morning, he couldn't be sure, but he thought he saw the rig in the distance.

He lifted the binocs strapped around his collar and looked. Definitely a smudge, thick and dark. He glimpsed the movement of a rising plume. Pulling the sound-powered mouthpiece closer, he pressed the button. "Bridge, Port Lookout."

He released, and Lee Vincent, an E-4 operations specialist, replied, "Bridge, aye."

"Vinnie, I've got black smoke on the horizon bearing three-*fife*-zero."

"Understand, smoke on horizon at three-five-zero degrees."

A momentary pause, while Vincent relayed the message, then the line clicked as someone keyed a handheld.

"Port lookout, this is the officer of the deck. Good eyes there."

"Thank you, sir," replied Red.

"Now look alive. We're expecting debris in the water… and bodies. Could even be survivors. Anything you see you report at once. Other vessels, helos, anything. There's a large rescue effort underway."

"Roger that, sir."

A faint click and Vincent came back in whispered tones, "Hey Red, you make sure to do your job now."

"Yeah," Red replied. "Damn junior grade gets on my nerves."

"Give Morrison time," said Vincent, "He'll figure it out."

"Doubt that. At his age he shoulda made lieutenant by now." Red lifted the binocs to his eyes. "Is he on the other side of the bridge or something? You know he'll call us out if you keep chattering." He searched the water between the bow and horizon.

"He's stepped outside. Having a look for himself," said Vincent.

"The captain on the bridge?"

"Not yet. Maybe down in CIC."

"Negative," came another voice. It was OS2 Gabriel, sitting a radar scope down in CIC, the Combat Information Center. One deck below the bridge and connected by a stairway, the CIC served as a hub for all tactical data, organizing info so the command staff could act quickly and decisively.

"Well, he's not on the bridge," Vincent repeated. "Sure he's not down there, Gabe? Maybe over in sonar or something?"

"I relayed that smoke to CIC, you morons," Gabriel continued. "If the captain was here, he would've hopped to the bridge already. I know how to do my job too, y'know."

"Well somebody needs to let the old man know," Red explained. "That's the rig out there burning. We'll reach it within an hour."

"I'll suggest that to Morrison," said Vincent, "If he ever hauls his ass back in here."

"Just don't want crap rolling down onto us," Red explained.

"How 'bout I say..." Vincent cleared his throat and whispered in falsetto, "Loooootenant Junior Grade *Morrisssson*, port lookout suggests we notify the captain, *sir*."

Red grinned. "Yeah, twenty bucks if you do."

"Starboard lookout, you got anything?" asked Gabe.

The reply was a distinct Boston accent, "Nah. Just the ships that came along with us. And a Golf Uniform Eleven."

Gabriel gave a slight chuckle. "Roger that."

Red interjected, "Hey, bridge you gonna report that bogey?"

Vincent answered, "Look, I was a seaman recruit, straight outta A school, okay."

"Yeah, but has anybody tried it on Morrison yet?" asked Red, "Go ahead, Vinnie, see if he knows what a *gull* is."

Gabe interjected, deciding to rein the younger sailors in, "You guys shut it so I can do my job. Aft lookout, you got anything?"

There was no reply.

"Aft lookout, CIC."

Still nothing.

Finally, Gabe barked, "Smitty, wake the hell up!"

"Uh… Aft lookout, aye." Smith's voice was thick and groggy.

"Yeah," Gabriel came back, "you got anything back there?"

"Hold on." A long pause and then, "Anything in particular? You see a blip on your radar?"

Gabriel's sigh came through first, loud enough they all heard, then he said, "No, but if we want shore leave at next port, we better not screw up. Definitely not today. We're coming up on that *Piper Alpha* rig."

"Shore leave's been cut short twice already," Smith replied, "And some of us were in the pub last night, but yeah, thanks for the tip."

Red chimed in, "Smitty, he's just trying to look out for us, bro. Keep in mind what we were briefed on." Then he added, "Remember, we gotta get you to third class. That is if you still want it."

"Just help me study, Red," came the reply. "I'll pass that exam next time, just need some help."

"You know I'll help..." Red scanned the ocean. "But Gabe is right. For now, we all better stay sharp. I'm seeing movement around that smoke." He used his binocs. "Helos. Got ships, hull down. Lots of 'em."

"Got confirmation on the 55," said Gabriel. "Starting to see 'em at the edge of my sweep. About six skunks, right at the edge. I'm gonna adjust my range." There was a brief silence while Gabe investigated the *skunks*, *S*urface *C*ontacts *UNK*nown, then he said, "Dammit, there's contacts all over this scope from 15 to 30 miles out. I shoulda spooled that range sooner. Gonna start marks for the DRT and see if we can pinpoint the rig. Vinnie, relay that for me, will ya? Damn… here I been crawling your asses."

Vincent replied, "I gotcha, Gabe. Officer of the deck is back on the bridge. All stations maintain radio protocol, while I report out." The line went silent, and everyone buckled down. Red kept scanning the port side and watching that dark plume inch its way closer.

His senses heightened; Red could see the fire in the distance. Ships that had been 'hull down', with only part of their profile above the horizon line, were now clearly on this side of that line. Red reported everything, as did his counterpart at starboard, and a renewed, no-nonsense chatter took hold.

Then, bearing 320 about 2000 yards out, Red caught a flash of movement. He stopped and slowly backtracked. He saw an unnatural glint, multicolored, bobbing between the waves. Was it debris? He pressed the binocs to his face and found it again.

There was a patch of color, like a small, jagged rainbow winking in and out of sight. The waves surrounding it were dappled with the faint light of a risen sun. He spied it again and the bobbing ceased as it grew and transformed into a rolling hump, followed by the graceful arc of a fin. Finally, a wide, strangely shaped tail broke the surface. It glimmered and pulled a streaming trail of droplets behind.

The tail spread in a wide fluke. A translucent strip marked its scalloped terminal edge, while iridescent webbing sloped down to merge into prismatic, silver scales.

Red was dumbstruck. What the hell kind of fish was that? Too big and colorful for any he'd seen and nothing like a whale or dolphin either. It flicked once, scattering water like a jackpot of dimes, then dove straight down.

Red stayed with that spot. It was probably nothing, but bodies in the water were chum for fish. He grabbed the mouthpiece to report.

Before he could, Red felt a tap on his shoulder. He eased his binoculars down, irked by the intrusion. Furrowing his brow, he turned and frowned at Ortiz. "Yeah?"

Ortiz motioned 'give' with both hands. "I was told to relieve you."

"Why?" Red pulled the strap over his head and carefully set the binocs on a metal storage box. "I just took post two hours ago."

Ortiz flashed a grin and wiggled his ears. "Your chance to shine," he said. He picked up the binocs, did a casual inspection and adjusted for his vision. "The old man just briefed oncoming officers and chiefs. Wants both SAR swimmers to suit up."

Red took off his headset and pulled a second strap from his neck. This one held the small chest-plate where the hinged arm of the mouthpiece was mounted. He felt a nervous thrill as he handed it to Ortiz, eager to suit up and possibly get in the water.

"Roger that," he finally blurted. He was about to head below when he remembered. He pointed out to sea. "Spotted smoke about ten degrees to port, on the horizon, that'll be the rig."

"Gotcha," said Ortiz. "Oil rig ahead. Anything else?"

"Just keep an eye out for debris, bodies, anything unusual." He paused to consider, then added, "There's a really weird fish out there. About 2000 yards out, bearing 320 when I spotted it."

Ortiz perked up. "Sturgeon. Bet your next paycheck."

"I don't think so."

"Sea bass."

"Ain't a stupid sea bass. Just keep your eyes open maybe you'll discover a new species."

"Mermaid." Ortiz smiled and took his post. "A really .." He put his palms on his chest, then moved them about a foot out. "...really big ... *big* hearted mermaid."

Red gave a quick two fingered salute. "I had it, you got it." He turned to go.

In no time Red was suited up and ready. "I'm clearing you to go," said the hospital corpsman, "But you're expected to know your limitations. I know you haven't slept in 24 hours."

"I'm good," Red insisted. "Just let me do my job."

The corpsman looked to the captain. "Sir, you've got the final say on this."

Commander Egan looked at Red with steel gray eyes. "Petty officer, don't make us regret this. From what I've heard, it's very unlikely you'll be pulling any survivors from the water. If you go in, I want to be sure you make it back. Don't want any of my crew added to the casualties of this mess."

"Yes sir, Captain." Red saluted, though he wasn't exactly in uniform anymore.

Egan returned the salute and made to go. "I'm heading to the bridge. Report to the riggers and stage in case you're needed."

"Aye, sir."

Red waited until the old man was gone. He turned to the corpsman. "Thanks, Whitzler."

"You can thank me by not doing anything stupid. Good luck, Red."

Red nodded and headed for the deck.

The morning was mostly uneventful. Until he was called on, Red was allowed to sit propped against the ship's hull. He managed to catch a few hours of sleep that way. Then around 1100 hours, he got his chance.

"Port lookout reports a body in the water bearing 280," said Petty Officer Reynolds. The 2nd class Boatswain's Mate was on the JL circuit, relaying information from the lookouts to Red. "About 100 yards out."

Red took a pair of binoculars to see for himself. He spotted it right away. Floating with face up and arms out to the side, the body wasn't moving. "He's unconscious."

The rig captain motioned to Red. "Get in position."

Red handed the binocs over to a crewmate and stood on the edge of the deck while the rigger conducted a final check of his gear. He donned the rescue strop, and the tending line was attached to his side. The rig captain called up Captain Egan for approval to deploy.

After a brief exchange, the crew was given the go-ahead. With the rescue strop in place, Red was lowered into the water. Once immersed, he swam out of the rig, cleared his mask, and gave the hand signal that he was okay. Red swam for the injured man, the tending line attached to his body harness spooling out behind as it fed from the reel.

Within a minute he had reached the body, ready to reach around so that the injured oiler would stay elevated as the men on the deck pulled them in.

But as he reached for the oiler, the man submerged forcefully, as if yanked from beneath. Red dove, his tending line following him under. Then the body turned, and he saw that it was gone from the waist down. The man was already dead.

Then Red saw something else, a murky silhouette within the blood clouded waters, right below the dead oilman. His mind grappled with this image, trying to make sense of it, while struggling to control his own fight-or-flight reflex. Through his watersuit, Red felt the sea temperature drop several degrees. His hackles raised even as his stomach knotted into a ball of fear, both instinctive and familiar. *Supernatural*, thought Red. *Whatever it is, that thing is pure evil.*

Holding to the man's arm was a creature like nothing Red had ever seen. The lower half was like the tail of a fish, while the torso was not-quite-human. It gripped the man's wrist with one scaly, webbed claw and the man's throat with the other. It pulled the body in toward its face and began to feast.

Red recognized the creature from earlier. The same iridescent scales, the same fin upon its back, and that uniquely scalloped tail. He wondered for an instant how such a thing, obviously a sea denizen, hadn't picked up on his presence. Then he noticed its ferocious bites, as it tore out chunks of flesh from the oiler. This thing was in the throes of a feeding frenzy. *Might be the one advantage I need.* Red kicked himself downward and, hardly thinking, reached across to unsheathe his swimming knife.

The creature flipped over, pushing its meal down, leaving its own back exposed. It was so ravenous, so focused on its prey, it had yet to see Red.

Red saw his chance and took it. He kicked his flippers to push himself within striking distance and drove the knife deep into the creature's back, opposite of where the heart should be. The water clouded with thick, purplish blood. The creature turned to face him. As it did, Red jerked his knife free, knowing he would need it. This was not over.

If this was a mermaid, then it was nothing like the descriptions. It was no beautiful half woman from the waist up, though it could very well be female. The thing had pale green skin and two noticeable breasts. Its mouth was open, exposing piranha-like teeth, sharp and crowded. Its eyes were viridian with vertically slitted pupils, and its hair floated in thick ropes of dark green, like seaweed crowning its head.

Slender arms shot up toward him, the forearms scaled in the same armor that covered most of its skin. Red slashed across a reaching palm, slicing it open and tearing the webbing stretched between the long, outstretched fingers.

The creature pulled its hand back, clearly not expecting such a show of resistance. The apex predator was suddenly surprised to find itself matched in its own territory. It made a sound like a startled porpoise, a high-pitched squeal marked with chattering clicks.

Before the thing could regain its composure, Red swam past, knife in one hand. He reached for the corpse as it slowly drifted down and managed to catch it by a cold, dead wrist.

He was preparing to surface and signal the crew to reel him in, when the creature bit through his tending line and descended on him.

Red kicked himself forward, meeting the thing halfway. He struck with his knife again, slicing across its breasts. So much blood filled the water that he could barely see. The creature grabbed at his throat, but he brought the knife up again, burying it in the thing's abdomen. Red kicked away from the beast, leaving his blade in its belly. It bared its teeth and pursued. Though terribly wounded, it let out a deafening screech, refusing to give up.

Red had weakened it. But even weighed down by the corpse he clung to, he was still able to outswim the creature. He breached and scanned frantically for the severed tending line. He saw it, drifting, and not that far away. The crew had surely felt it go slack. If he didn't hurry, they would prep the other swimmer to deploy and rescue *him*.

He quickly swam to the drifting line and took hold with his free hand. He looked back to see his shipmates cheering him on. Red looped the line around his palm and nodded for them to retrieve him. They began turning the spool. Red felt the line grow taut and then his body forcefully pulled through the water. He turned his back to the ship, allowing the line to drag him along while he clutched the dead man's wrist.

As the men on the boat worked to retrieve Red, they noticed a school of small fins darting across the water, following him in. But they didn't notice the churning cloud he left behind. A single, larger fin, arcing in a wounded spasm that then disappeared into waters dark with blood and slick with oil.

Chapter 4

One week later, July 14, 1988
Rosyth, Scotland

In the aftermath, the ship had returned to Scotland, but not to catch up on their interrupted R&R, which the crew still desperately needed. For one, they'd had debris and a few bodies to deliver. There were also lots of questions to answer. Local officials were escorted aboard and debriefed with prepared statements, while Naval Intelligence seemed to play both sides, advising the officers on one hand, then turning right around to sequester individual crewmen and grill them in what felt like borderline interrogations.

Finally, it was Red's turn to be questioned in the repurposed crew's lounge. As the Master at Arms led the way, McCraith was surprised to see a Marine posted outside the door. The old salt mumbled something to the Marine, who then took one step aside. McCraith swallowed hard and prepared himself. The Master at Arms opened the door and motioned for the younger man to enter. Once Red entered, the Master at Arms simply closed the door from outside, as if throwing the sailor to the proverbial lions.

In the center of the room was a small table and two chairs. In one chair, opposite Red, sat a man wearing an indistinct uniform, dark and devoid of any rank or rating insignia. Then a pin on the man's collar caught the young man's eye—a gold and red dragon, nothing more. The man's hair was buzzed and gray, his skin tanned as old leather, with a jagged pink scar along the curve of one cheekbone. His eyes were like blue ice. Without standing, the man nodded for the young sailor to be seated.

While Petty Officer McCraith took his seat, the other man kept his clipboard angled, so the young sailor couldn't read across the table. He made a show of ticking items on a legal pad and started with the obvious, "Son, why aren't you at Annapolis? Or part of a SEAL team right now? Hell, you had the chops for both. I've gone over your records—test scores are off the chart, psych eval aligns perfectly, and physically you're top notch. So what gives? What made you crack?"

Boatswain's Mate Third Class Thomas 'Red' McCraith held back a sigh. That same old question. Phrased differently from time to time, but it always came down to one thing: Why did he choose to live below what others considered his 'potential'?

He looked the man in the eyes. "Sir, those records, test scores, and psychological evals can tell you a lot, but not everything. So maybe *you* can gauge the difference between *cracking* and making a decision."

He could sense the man forming a rebuke, so he held up his hands. "Don't mean a bit of disrespect, sir. So please just hear me out." Taking a slow breath, he went on. "For as long as I can remember, I wanted to serve, like my daddy and my grandpa. I wanted to make a difference without wasting time to do it. I went enlisted, like they did. Wanted to see the world while I'm young. As for college, I've got the G.I. Bill for later, but after 18 years I was ready to get outta podunk Georgia and make my own way."

The older man grunted, squinting with those ice-blue eyes and making a note on his pad. "Go on," he grumbled.

Red put a finger to the rating badge on his sleeve. "Believe me, I get tired of explaining why I left the farm for this, and why I dropped out of BUDS. But my family tries to respect my decisions. I could've joined the Marines, like Grandpa, but I wanted to serve in the Navy like Daddy, and I know I could've completed SEALs training, but ... in *that* moment I knew I'd stepped from where I was meant to be. I know everybody thinks I made a huge mistake, but I had to get out and back to sea."

Studying his notepad, the man wrote and replied absently, "You were too eager, in my opinion." He looked back up at the red-haired Petty Officer. "Which I know is because of your friend who died on the *Stark*, right before you dropped out. They call it 'survivor's guilt', in case you didn't know." He squinted at the sailor, as if trying to read him, then took another tack: "Or maybe it was fear. Maybe you thought we were about to go to war and finally realized being a SEAL might get you a front row seat to the action?" The weathered veteran paused, clearly waiting to see if Red took the bait.

"I'm not a coward, *that* should be obvious from the reports and exams, but even before what happened to the *Stark*, I wasn't all gung-ho looking for someone to kill. Matter of fact, I'd actually prefer not to—since we clearly don't know exactly *who* needs killing. And even though you didn't ask, I'll tell you straight: I think our President is wrong about Iraq. Regardless of our current support of their war with Iran, and despite Hussein's insistence that the *Stark* was a tragic accident, I don't trust or believe Saddam for a second. That monster knew what he was doing." Red watched as that sunk in.

"I'm not here to debate politics, the decisions of our Commander in Chief, or our alignment with the lesser of two evils," said the man. "The topic is *you*. So tell me what you hope to accomplish in your present role."

Setting his jaw, Red continued, "I figure on a ship like this, I'm doing my part. And I'll probably never have to draw down on a man. Especially if I'm not sure he needs it. I mean, I would if I had to, if it were him or me, or one of my shipmates. But I'd rather not have to."

The man's blue eyes narrowed as he shoved a word in, "Son, the military isn't looking for trigger-happy sociopaths, and men who go to war know what it's about, seeing friends die and taking human life. Be that as it may, when you signed up, you agreed to do what has to be done and to follow lawful orders."

Nodding, the younger man relaxed his tone in deference. "Yes sir, I know that. America and the US Navy both have my full allegiance. All I'm saying is I wanted to be a part of something bigger than myself. To be there for my country when it needs me. I also decided I don't want to kill people for some political agenda or because the world needs a scapegoat. Not if I don't have to. That's all."

Those blue eyes stared, unblinking, as the man held his pen to his bottom lip and studied Red intently. "Kind of sounds like you should've joined the Peace Corps."

Chagrined, Red scratched behind an ear. "Yeah, that's what Grandpa said."

The man shrugged. "...or the Coast Guard."

Red shook his head and grimaced. "And that would be Daddy."

Writing again, the strange, gray haired man kept his clipboard at a tilt. "You're definitely no coward. Twice you've encountered things you can't explain and each time you kept your senses about you."

Red frowned. "Yeah, exactly how much do you know about that?"

"We interviewed your shipmates, Ortiz and Smith, and the riggers handling your lines during the search and rescue. They wouldn't tell us much. Kept saying they weren't sure about what they may have seen."

The man leaned in. "But son, we've been putting out fires all over the globe for centuries now, so we know how to get to the truth. Even when others refuse to believe their eyes and are disinclined to speak. Before we get to that, though, I've got to know..." The man leaned back again and stared at Red, no judgment in his eyes, just honest curiosity. "Even though you rang the bell, you were still given a choice of ratings, why did you go back undesignated? Then strike for Boatswain's Mate when testing for third class?"

Red was curious about what kind of fires the man was talking about. Since that larger topic was shelved for now, he got right to the point. "Wanted to get my hands dirty. Do the grunt work no one else wants. I know, what was I thinking? But honestly, I enjoy it. It's mostly hard, sweaty work; like the farm. But I'm proud to be a Deck Dog."

Lines creased the man's leathery face as he finally smiled. "Called 'em Deck Apes when I was at sea."

Red shrugged. "Either way, we're what's left of the sailors of old; man the wheel, climb to the crow's nest, secure that line, swab the deck. Maybe we're crass and simple to some folks, but those men are my brothers."

"I see." The man seemed on the verge of standing, which would signal the end of their meeting. Instead, he shifted his weight, reached down to the open case by his chair, and put his clipboard away. "Now then, tell me straight…" He came back with a manila folder and set it on the table. Then he pulled up one corner to slip out a single photograph—an 8x10, low resolution, and just a bit blurred. Pushing it over, he asked, "What do you make of this?"

"That's a banshee." The young sailor passed the photo back.

The man took out a second photograph.

Red studied it. "A mermaid," he said. "They're nothing like Daryl Hannah in that Tom Hanks movie, I can tell you that."

"I'm sure you can," the older man replied, smiling again. An ease had settled between them, as if the man had found what he was searching for in the young sailor.

"They confiscated my camera after they took in that body and started questioning me. So that first photo is mine," Red explained. "But not the second one. It looks like the same creature, though. How did you get it?"

Dodging the question, the man posed his own, "When your chain of command asked about your knife, why did you..."

"Tell them the truth?" Red finished for him.

"You had to know they wouldn't believe you."

Red crossed his pale, freckled arms and leaned in. "It was the second time inside twenty-four hours I had seen something unexplainable. I figured *someone* had to know something, and I figured the quickest way to find that someone was to use the only avenue I had, the truth. So I told them about the mermaid, with my knife still in its belly. When they called b.s. on that, I told them about the banshee. Which I guess is why Ortiz and Smitty got interrogated."

"You didn't worry that your camera would be confiscated? Or your shipmates be put under the microscope?"

Red shrugged. "Figured if they took my camera it was just further proof I'd stumbled onto something. I saw those bite marks all over that corpse. I knew they weren't made by any known species. Hell, I watched the thing that did it. As for Ortiz and Smitty, I figured they'd be grilled either way, had no more to lose than I did."

When the man spoke again, it was with a tone of practiced authority, "Actually, those are the teeth marks of a cowfish, a shark found in these waters. It's something of a scavenger and was taking advantage of an opportunity. Good thing you were there to fight it off. The family can have closure and that man a decent burial."

Red's eyes widened, then he smiled. "Okay, so that's the official story. Guess I'll just have to go along with it." He studied the man and went for broke. "Sir, you've heard everything I know. I've answered every question thoroughly and honestly. Now you tell me something: who are you and what do you *really* do?"

The man put the photos and the folder away. "I'm a recruiter for an elite group of soldiers. Like I said, we put out fires. Not exactly burning oil platforms. Let's just say that sometimes, when things like this happen, certain other things get stirred up. We take care of those."

"Sir, that banshee might've been a harbinger, but I don't think it actually caused all of this."

The man shrugged. "The world is more unstable than you realize. The actions of other countries are sending shockwaves across the waters. Oil starts wars. And if a banshee gets stirred, so do other things."

Red blinked as the man's words finally sank in. "A recruiter? And you're talking to me. Is this an interview or...?"

The man pursed his lips, as if carefully choosing his words. Finally, he answered, "Not an interview, per se. But it *is* an invitation. You show a lot of promise. Tons of potential. I'd like to put it to the highest possible use. So, what do you think?"

Red wasn't as straightforward. He fumbled over his words, trying to express himself and answer honestly. "Sir, this...*invitation*, if that's what we're calling it, well...it feels...*right* somehow. Down in my gut, I mean."

The recruiter furrowed his brow. "I'm going to need a little more than that."

Red sighed. "I feel like I've been running—for a long time. First I thought I just needed to get out of my hometown. So I joined up. And when my first XO tapped me to look into SEALs, I thought maybe that was my path." He shook his head. "But it never seemed to fit. And I know this'll sound cheesy as hell, but I've been running from or running toward something, and I'm thinking it might be the same thing but at different times."

Intrigued by that, the recruiter prompted, "Go on."

"My destiny, sir. I've run from it, then looked for it. Got scared and hid from it. Guess I can't hide anymore, and now that it's here I don't even want to." He shrugged with his hands out to his sides, palms up. "I was in the least likely place for it to find me, chipping paint and barnacles, and yet it did."

The man rubbed his chin. "Destiny is a strange way to put it. I'm not offering fame or glory, not even a pay raise. Thirteen is as covert as it gets. We take most of our achievements, our secrets, to the grave. So don't fool yourself into thinking this is something other than what it really is. The offer stands, but this is totally your choice, and I'd like you to make it carefully with eyes wide open. We don't press anyone into service."

Red took that in, then replied, "Sir, I'm not saying I'm a victim of fate. But I do think I've got a role to play on a larger scale. Or maybe just a different one. I think it's the reason I chose the path I did. To ultimately get me where I really need to be. When they pulled me up onto the ship, and I had what was left of that poor guy, with teeth marks all over him, I just wanted to find another knife and dive back in. Put a stop to that nonsense. But it's even bigger than that. There's something huge going on in the world. Like a storm coming. Somebody's got to stop it."

The man nodded slowly, as if gauging Red's reaction. "Good instincts. Let's just say the Middle East is a powder keg. We've got our hands full right now, and from what I've seen it's just going to get worse."

"So maybe I can help."

"I believe you can. Our scout believes you can, or else he wouldn't have recommended you."

Red frowned. "Scout?"

"On temporary assignment to your ship. He's part of your 'Snoopy Team'. Lieutenant Junior Grade Morrison."

"He took the mermaid photo," Red realized. The Snoopy Team consisted of a handful of crewmen, activated when there was intel to gather. When Russian ships drew close for impromptu races, or other random encounters.

"Morrison thinks you're a fit. I think you're a fit. What do you think?" The man stood. "You said you don't want to draw down on a man, but you may have to before this is over. At this point the question is somewhat rhetorical, but let me ask anyway—what about an inhuman? Like a banshee? Creatures of myth and lore that are simply living in another dimension and sometimes cross over into ours, what some people would call 'supernatural', got any problem killing those?"

Red was dumbstruck for a moment, as the weight of it all sunk in. "You mean all that's real? Mermaids, sea monsters… I actually saw what I saw, and I'm not slipping mentally?"

Leathery skin creased in mirth as the recruiter laughed. "Son, you didn't think that for a second."

"I honestly don't know, sir." Red ran a wide, deck-calloused hand over his short, red hair. "I'd been over a day without sleep. Was tired, running on raw adrenaline. I didn't *believe* I was slipping, but I couldn't entirely rule it out and, for a while there, I was wondering if our interview might be a psych assessment in disguise. But you're telling me that folklore has its basis in truth. The supernatural is real?"

A single nod. "Absolutely real, and often the creatures are even more deadly than the legends portray. So the question remains: do you have a problem sending lead downrange at a shape-shifter or a dragon? Or, if necessary, at any humans responsible for summoning them or who have surrendered their souls to demonic forces?"

Following the man's lead, Red stood up, straight-backed and solemn, to show he recognized and respected the gravity of the moment. "No sir, no issues with that whatsoever. Like dropping a buck or a wild boar back home." Then, sensing the need for a bit of levity, he added, "Just don't expect me to eat 'em."

Grinning, the man said, "You might need more than a deer rifle. So is that a *yes* I'm hearing? You want to be part of one of the most elite task forces on the planet?"

"You are definitely hearing a yes. I'd be honored to join your new Task Force to battle creatures from beyond."

The man shook his head. "We're old, recruit. Older than your great grandpa, but I do feel we're coming into our own here of late." He put out a hand. "Designation is 13."

Red took the proffered hand. "Good thing I ain't superstitious."

A wink and a nod. "Give it time." The recruiter reached into his leather case again and pulled out an envelope. "Here are your other photographs. Minus any that might arouse suspicion of course. You won't be going back aboard your ship either. We're sending someone after your personal belongings, and then you disappear for a while."

"Will I see my friends again?"

"You won't exactly be the same if you do, but maybe." He smiled. "You should hear the way they bragged on you. How they hoisted you in while a school of sharks followed, and you never even flinched. Just held on to the body with one hand and the line with the other."

"What about Smitty?" Red remembered his promise. "I was supposed to tutor him, help him get his crow. His first chevron."

The recruiter cocked his head. "Loyalty. I respect that. I'll see that someone gives him quality tutelage. Beyond that, I think I can pull a string, make sure he gets enough points to bump him over if he still doesn't quite hit the mark."

"I'd appreciate that. Oh, and I reckon you should know, so I don't come off like I think I'm bulletproof..." He shook his head and admitted, "Reason I never flinched was 'cause I never even *saw* any sharks."

"Of course not." The man fastened the latch on his case. "You were too focused on other things."

"Wasn't thinking about that mermaid, either. I was just trying to hold on to — well what was left of that oil rigger and to the line."

"Exactly, son. You were holding the line."

Chapter 5

July 1988 - August 1990

Red's belongings were packed up and delivered by none other than Lieutenant Jr. Grade Morrison, who simply put out a hand and said, "Inter Caelum Et Infernum."

Red reached for the proffered hand with a puzzled reply, "Between Heaven and Hell?"

Morrison's eyes widened. "A hick that knows Latin. Maybe I made a good call."

"I'm an educated hick, sir. Thanks to a grandpa who loved Latin and served in World War Two."

As they finished the handshake, Morrison said, "Welcome to Team Spooky."

Red found the next few years to be a blur. First, he was whisked away, temporarily assigned to the nearest unit, which meant acting as a junior troop ammo guy, doing grunt work no one else wanted. Red secretly enjoyed it, but before he could settle in, it was off to Quantico for the entire month of August, where he completed the indoctrination course for JTF13. It was an eye-opening experience that provided strange and intriguing context for what he'd seen in the field.

First he learned about the facts behind the creatures of folklore: gargoyles, golems, gremlins, demons, dryads, and dragons were covered in levels of detail beyond anything he'd read in a book or seen in a movie. There were even actual photos and wartime film footage of sea monsters, reanimated corpses, fairies, shape-shifters, and nightwalkers who drained blood from the living—all the ancient legends brought to life in unbelievable detail.

Augmenting the training material of classified documents, photos, and film were artifacts recovered from the battlefield, ancient texts, and relics of antiquity passed down through the ages. These were kept behind vacuum-sealed, bulletproof glass, often in cases with holy symbols worked into the surface and prayers inscribed on their marble or wooden bases. There were original texts of 'Book of the Watchers' and 'The Book of Giants'.

All the displays were crucial in impressing the true nature of reality, but the main thrust of the course was to train recruits in how to battle these monsters from other realms. Red learned that the most obvious choice, to use supernatural means, was the least desirable, for a few reasons. One, if holy petitions were uttered, the person using them better have a faith to match or the demons would have a field day with the poor soul. Two, if a dark spell was used, the creature might actually derive more power from the utterance.

Best bet, therefore, was always more firepower. Throw enough lead, cold steel, or gunpowder at the problem until the creature, or the fleshly form a demonic spirit had been forced to take, was simply ripped to shreds or blown apart.

After the month-long course, Red's instructor graduated the class and sent them off with orders in hand. "Fresh meat for the hellions!" was how the Master Sergeant put it. But first, for Red and a few others, it was off to Airborne school. Three weeks of training to get jump qualified. Then, for a while at least, he was back to sea, sometimes as part of a conventional force, at others on temporary assignment with the JTF.

In spring of '89, at the urging of his superiors, he was given the choice of a new rating and completed A School for Intelligence Specialists. Then, toward the end of that year, he found himself steaming south from Mayport, Florida to Panama on the *USS Vreeland*, FF-1068. Originally launched as a destroyer escort (DE-1068), the ship was redesignated as a frigate in July of '75. She measured about 450 feet with 45 feet across her beam. A decent sized warship with a complement of over 280 crewmen, again exactly the kind of ship the young Intelligence Specialist was accustomed to. He was part of an embedded JTF team during 'Operation Just Cause'.

"Remind me again why we're standing watch on this fantail with an M16," Red said to the Marine Corporal, as he relieved the man to take mid-watch.

"I know, right," said Corporal Duffy, a New Yorker with the stereotypical attitude. "Been up and down this coast and ain't seen the first Facu-mama."

Red laughed. "I think they called it a Yacumama."

"Whatever," Duffy replied. "An anaconda with horns? Gimme a break. What are we, pest control now?" He started walking and nodded to Red. "Have fun, ya' hillbilly."

"Grew up near the swamp," Red reminded Duffy as he walked away. "Ain't no hills in South Georgia."

Duffy didn't look back, just gave him the one-finger salute as he headed for his bunk.

"Love you too, Duff!" Red shot back, which earned him the two handed one-finger salute. Red smiled and checked his weapon, then put eyes on the water and set his mind for the next four hours.

He didn't really expect anything. They'd left Mayport to provide support on the northern coast, mostly just steaming east and west for the better part of a month. There were three other JTF members aboard beside

Red—a fire team, nothing more. But there was apparently enough smoke on this Yacumama creature to get the brass at 13 to at least sniff it out, see if there was anything besides the typical rumor mill and one grainy photo.

Still, they took the most reasonable course and committed the smallest force possible. If there was more to it, they'd send in reinforcements. Until then, a Corporal, two Lance Corporals, and 'fresh-meat McCraith' would do.

Red completely understood and would have made the same decision were he in their position. Of course, that didn't mean he had to like it. More than anything, he just felt useless. The JTF detachment couldn't even support the crew in menial cleanup, since the round-the-clock watches took all their time.

So when the creature finally did show, at around 0200 hours, Red thought at first he was seeing a sub. He was about to radio it in, when the water seemed to rise in a great swell, right next to him. Then the horned monster reared from the ocean and opened its maw, exposing rows of daggered teeth.

In a single smooth motion, Red swung the M16A2 to his shoulder, thumbed off the safety, selected for burst, and opened fire. He lit up the fantail, putting 3 rounds in the creature's head as it poised to strike.

It lunged, forcing Red to jump aside. Somehow, he kept his feet under him as the monster's head hit the deck. It writhed in fury and pain, undulating back toward the ocean. Red kept his senses and held his weapon up and away from the ship. He thumbed the switch back to safety, keeping an eye on the wriggling creature.

Red heard the aft lookout yelling at him. He ignored the sailor as he adjusted his position and gauged that of the serpent. It had slithered back toward the ocean, but instead of clearing the rail, it shot between.

Like the hinged fangs of its mouth, the large horn—center of its forehead—tilted back, resting against its scaled hide. The two smaller ones on either side did the same. This allowed the snake to slip between the deck and lower set of rails. Then its retreat abruptly halted as its girth lodged it tight, preventing further passage.

The giant snake had effectively pinned itself in place. A full two thirds of the creature now moved side to side, tracking with the ship as it was dragged atop the waves. The remaining third, including its bloody head, turned back toward the ship and slowly began to rise. There was no way for the creature to disengage. It would now stay with the ship until its end.

In the dim light, Red noticed the exit wound, a punctured left eye. He vowed better placement next chance he got. Preparing for the snake's second strike, he backed against the superstructure and waited.

The Yacumama caught sight of him with its remaining eye. It rushed then jerked to a halt, wriggling in vain as it realized again it was pinned. It opened its mouth, hissing at Red in anger, it exposed its fangs and dozens of teeth—like blades of sharpened bone. It reared to strike.

Red put his finger on the trigger. Two bursts, center of the gaping mouth. Lead ripped through the creature's brain, blowing off the top of its skull. The shots also detached the horn, which clattered aftward where it stopped at the edge of the ship. The monster reeled to one side and fell in an avalanche of flesh. Blood spilled from the shattered skull, gushing across the deck and onto Red's boots.

"Ooh-Rah!" came a hearty voice from his right.

Red turned. "Hey, Duff. Sorry I didn't leave you any action. What brings you back up here anyway?"

"Couldn't sleep. Get all tingly when the creep show starts." Duff gazed out into the night. "Think there's more where this came from?"

Before that possibility could be explored, the Panamanian Defense Forces were overwhelmed, and Noriega surrendered. The Yacumama carcass, including the severed horn, was put on ice and crated up, but not before Red discretely skinned a patch of torn hide from the creature. Once the *Vreeland* returned to home port, the team disbanded, the crate was sent to Intel, and Red was off to school again.

His scores at A school along with his encounter with the Yacumama earned him a ticket into C school. There was no B school, which never ceased to amaze him. Whether intentional or not, the Navy seemed to have a real knack for red-tape and misdirection. Sailors chosen to develop and refine the skills of their rating went straight from A to C. Go figure.

He finished in the Spring. Once again, his performance got the attention of the higher ups at Intel. He was tapped to start immediately as part of Intel HQ, but for the first time since joining 13, Red balked.

"Will I have to man a computer day in and day out? And will I get any sea time at all?"

The Marine scrunched his weathered, age-lined face and gave a carefully worded reply, "Of course you'll get field time. But if we're gonna fast track you, you need to get up to speed as soon as possible."

Red swallowed hard. He'd already spent the better part of two years in training of one kind or another. It was making him cagey. "All due respect, sir, but I'd rather get more sea time under my belt." He touched the sea service ribbon on his uniform to make it clear.

At that, the grizzled Marine, a Chief Warrant Officer W-5, barked, "Petty Officer McCraith, this is an opportunity we're offering here!"

Red kept his tone respectful, "I assure you, sir, I appreciate that offer. Just hear me out."

The man snorted and said, "Go ahead, I'm listening."

Red turned his palms out in supplication, his voice sincere. "Sir, you didn't start out where you are. When you first enlisted, the early years, what were they like?"

The man shook his head but couldn't suppress a chuckle. "A glorious mess is what they were. There was this one time we had to battle it out with a bunch of reanimated corpses. Zombies for lack of a better word. Had a bunch of old, unreliable ammo. Thought it was the end..." His eyes narrowed as his voice dropped to a whisper, his mind suddenly drifting across time, "...but it was only the beginning."

"So don't take that from me," Red pleaded. "The day is bound to come I'll be more than happy to park my old bones, no offense, behind a desk. But not yet." He looked away, recalling memories of his own.   "I want to smell the salt again. Feel the breeze at 36 knots while I'm standing on the fantail. The waves while I'm strapped in my rack during twenty-foot seas. Or trying to keep my footing while the ship rides up one wave and then falls, shaking like hell as the next one crashes over, spray breaking across every window on the bridge."

"Don't forget to throw a sea-devil or two into those little scenarios," said the Marine. "I trust you haven't forgotten that Yacumama. The thing could've killed you. Keep in mind, too, you'll probably lose more than a few friends along the way. Or be among the lost."

Red nodded. "A risk you were willing to take. And one I'll never back down from."

The old Warrant Officer sighed. "Okay, dumbass. Have it your way. But don't hold your breath when you're ready for that cushy desk job. We might not be so keen to pull out a chair for you."

Red tried, but couldn't hold his tongue, "Another risk I'm willing to take... *sir*."

"McCraith, you're dismissed," the man said. As Red turned and walked away, the Marine added loudly, "Dumbass!"

Though the hint of a rescinded offer hung in the back of Red's mind, he knew he had more than an aptitude for intelligence work. He was also close enough to his two-year mark, and his scores high enough, to earn him another stripe and a seat at JTF's leadership course—a three-month training, again at Quantico.

This time the training was augmented with 'behind the scenes' access to things not shown to raw recruits. The newly frocked IS2 was given access to parts of the archive not available during the intro course. He found that, not only did the task force have a wealth of ancient texts and artifacts, they also had a few corpses.

The mummified head of a Nephilim was kept under a glass dome. With pale, white skin drawn tight across its skull, it sported a golden headband encrusted with precious gems. A mass of brittle, red hair was pulled back in a long braid. Its mouth, open wide in death, exposed double rows of molars.

Red stood slack-jawed at the exhibit. The head was the size of a ripe watermelon. According to the placard at its side, the giant was slain in a cave near Lovelock, Nevada. Standing nearly twelve feet tall, the creature had boasted its name was *Yalda Bahuth*, meaning 'Son of Chaos'. From a race of cannibalistic giants, which were nearly wiped out by the Paiute Indians (who called these ancient enemies Si-Te-Cah), the monster had caused years of trouble for the Task Force. Amazingly, a few of its descendants still survived.

This particular giant was killed in 1886 by a JTF operative, a young man by the name of Nikola Tesla. Part of JTF's Intelligence arm, he was traveling incognito for the singular purpose of slaying the creature with an experimental weapon of his own design. Aided by a local

Paiute tribal member, one 'Jack Wilson', also known as Wovoka, Tesla chased the giant to the mouth of the cave and let him have it with a prototypical weapon which was an elegant, fully functional, magnetic coilgun. The metal projectile had punched a hole right through the creature's chest, shredding its heart and severing its spine. Tesla cut off the thing's head with its own obsidian blade, to make sure it was dead.

There were other exploits by the young inventor, and most of them classified documents of the JTF. As for Wovoka, although he refused enlistment in JTF, the revered Paiute religious leader was often a source of information and was tapped for intel from time to time. Since he and Tesla were about the same age, both born in 1856, and both a bit eccentric, they became friends for life and often worked together as the Task Force had need.

Red was also amazed to discover the truth behind the bigfoot legends. How the creatures slipped in and out of our dimension, seemingly at will, and popped up all over the world. These reclusive creatures generally kept to themselves, but could be deadly if encountered. Bigfoot was known by many names across the globe: sasquatch, wendigo, yeti, yowie, xueren, almas, chimiset, chuchunaa, higabon. In the US it was also called wildman, skunk ape, swamp ape, and woodbugger. For all its encounters with the creature, the Task Force had only one specimen to date. Mounted and on display, it stood eight feet tall and sported thick, dark brown fur. It stood in the pose it held right before Teddy Roosevelt shot it through the left eyeball: one arm raised in a fist, snarling with its huge square incisors and long, pointed cuspids. The former President had encountered it shortly before he led the Rough Riders in the Battle of San Juan Hill. Once dead, the Task Force snuck it out of Cuba, no doubt pissing off Roosevelt, who'd wanted it stuffed and with his big game collection.

These were the things shared with enlisted members of the force. It wasn't that Officers were privy to more information, it was just different. As an Intelligence Specialist, Red was exposed to both, not as thoroughly as the higher ups, of course, but enough to give him a unique perspective.

Coming out of the leadership course, IS2 Thomas 'Red' McCraith was armed not only with the knowledge of what was out there and how to kill it, but also with the realization that there were layers upon layers of what was known, what was unknown, and the sobering fact that there were some things you simply never wanted to find out.

He graduated the course in August of 1990 and was finally sent back to sea, with the orders that would truly set the course of his life.

Chapter 6

August 6, 1990
JTF 13 outpost, Camp Lemonnier
1420 hours

The Djibouti government was allowing JTF13 a small corner from which to work. Just two small buildings, one for their equipment and workstations, the other to live in. 13 paid to connect the buildings with outside power and they brought in backup generators to keep the electronics running. It was an arrangement that could change at any time, given the on-going conflict in the nation.

Hunched at a monitor, Ensign Cassandra 'Cassie' Straub studied her latest video footage, trying to figure out what she was missing. It was there, but she couldn't quite put her finger on it.

There were three of the creatures. Merfolk, for lack of a better term, and all three were male. They showed clear hostility for one another, some sort of alpha-male dominance she suspected, yet they also seemed intent on the blurred patch of light beneath them.

The footage was from a surveillance probe, an unmanned submersible that searched for mines and passively tracked any craft which passed through its range. The technology was in a developmental phase, so data was often incomplete and less than optimal. The probe had returned to its docking bay in the shallows, where she retrieved it herself then transported it to the work building to examine its data.   Nothing   was allowed to connect directly with the small mainframe, so the data disk—a cutting edge version—had been removed to examine using her standalone computer.

Cassie paused the video then backed it up to watch again. The mermen obscured her line of sight, but there was clearly some movement within the glowing jagged line that ran diagonally across the screen. She frowned. Was there some sort of fissure in the seabed? Some volcanic activity undetected until now? It was too deep to be reflected sunlight. And the probe itself was coated in a black high impact polymer. It would reflect nothing and gathered most of its data passively; outgoing sonar was kept to a minimum, and it lacked even the smallest search beam to illuminate surroundings. If not for the glow shining from below the mermen, Cassie doubted the probe would've captured this video at all.

Though a JTF veteran, each discovery left her unsettled. Images of the strange encounters swirled in her mind. It was as if her subconscious knew some things were best left alone, and ancient, sleeping evil fit that bill. Like the grainy images rocking with the undercurrents of the Red Sea, her thoughts seemed adrift and hard to gather. She was missing something. What was it?

Then she noticed an odd sound mingled with the soft hum of the drone's propulsion system. She paused the video. Probably just the combined noise of other internal mechanisms, but she needed to be sure.

She watched it a third time, turning up the volume. There it was again. A chattering, almost like a bottlenose dolphin. Scanning the image, she looked for signs of the mammal, or any similar creature that would account for the sound. A shadow on the seabed or a shape along the periphery. Nothing. Then she realized what it must be and went back once again to verify.

She watched intently, volume up, paying attention to every squeal, chirp, and chatter, pairing them in her mind with the smallest gesture or slightest hint of facial expression. And just like that she had it.

She smiled as she matched the body language of the three fish-men with the sporadic chatter. This was their language! And this was either an argument or at the least an intense discussion. They were unsettled. Their motions along with the heated, though subdued chatter, indicated they were trying *not* to be heard. Clearly, they were frightened of the blurred light, or whatever was causing it. She watched as they conferred a final time, their need to establish dominance subdued by the perceived danger. Then they broke and swam in different directions, as though a decision had been reached.

Even after all this, she still felt a puzzle piece hadn't quite yet clicked into place. Something about the light troubled her in that way she'd learned never to ignore. The way the mermen acted proved it was important, an anomaly that JTF 13 simply must investigate.

She checked the coordinates superimposed in the lower left corner of the footage. Maybe she could program the probe to go back, leave its normal search pattern and dive closer for a better look. It was just so far north of the base, and deeper than the probes were designed to go. If the energy required to force it down and overcome the resultant pressure caused the batteries to deplete, the probe would be lost. And this was *her* project, her brainchild.

To make things worse, the timing was all wrong. No way was 13 going to divert resources for this. Not with Saddam Hussein flexing his muscles in Kuwait. Not to mention the fact that she had so little to go on. Just some chattering mermen clicking and pointing at an indistinct fissure of light.

Cassie either had to come up with a solid reason to prioritize that light or make some tangential appeal that would get her what she wanted in the process. Whatever she came up with, it would have to be fast. She'd be boarding the *Scorpius* soon, the Pegasus Class hydrofoil currently docked at Camp Lemonnier's pier, along with a squad of marines and sailors.

She slid the keyboard away and planted her elbows on the table, setting her chin in her hands. "Think Cassie." She closed her eyes and took a deep breath, initiating the ritual that allowed her to go beyond the rational and conjure her best and craziest ideas. As always, she started with the obvious, speaking each idea aloud:

"They won't send a diver. Not with so little to go on. And I don't want to risk losing a probe. So can I soup up the batteries?" Another deep breath. "Nope. Already maxed out and no time to research further. But what if I program one to go straight there, run deeper than usual, collect data only at that location, and then come back?"

She stood and opened her eyes, hands on the edge of the desk. "Too risky. May not maintain hull integrity at that depth." She clasped her hands behind her back and started pacing. "Could I program it to seek out one of our vessels on the return trip, so it doesn't have to travel so far? Maybe, but if it falls into enemy hands, I just compromised my team."

She sighed in frustration. There had to be some way to get what she wanted. What she knew in her bones the JTF *needed*. With world events escalating, emerging fires would surely dictate their orders. The deployment could quickly turn into the completely reactive approach that she downright despised. They needed to go on the offensive. Be proactive.

Cassie calmed herself again. That glowing fissure was going to remain a mystery until it was too late, unless she could appeal directly to their primary and secondary missions. She went over them again out loud, "The Primary Mission is to protect against Supernatural elements and forces arrayed against the United States military. The Secondary Mission is investigative. To understand the unknown, to reach into the dark and pull back the truth." Then it came to her.

She grinned, then started to laugh at the absurdity of her idea. It was crazy. All out lunacy. It was also the kind of thing that would appeal to the bad asses in the field and the data junkies back at Intel. It would work. It would get things moving exactly the way she wanted.

She ejected the disc and got to work.

Saxüru had been very patient, carefully biding his time as he tightened his grasp on the native creatures before summoning the supernatural. Satisfied his grip was secure, he finally took his staff and dug lines here and there along the seafloor, creating thin slices in the dimensional veil. This way the others could find their way through, often without even realizing they had done so.

He watched as the openings split wider on their own and continued to wait. Finally, when he was satisfied that others of his kind were passing back and forth without even knowing it, Saxüru summoned one of his horde—a scaled yet bearded creature, like a glorious unholy hybrid of fish and human. Down in the trenches, where the rift had opened to let him through, Saxüru sat upon his jagged ridge as one of his scaled minions approached and bowed. Its bedraggled mane touched the rocky floor as it spoke:

"Master, it has been far too long. But as ever, I am your willing servant."

Saxüru motioned him to rise and look around. "Gurax, do you not recognize this realm?"

The creature gazed about with slitted green eyes. It sniffed at the briny depths, drawing in huge streams of water. "At last, the world of man! It has opened to us. Master, what would you have me do first?" A grin split Gurax's face, revealing a mouthful of crowded, pointed teeth.

"Much time has passed," said Saxüru. "But indeed, the veil between worlds has once more been torn. Now come and hear my command, for we have work to do. And we dare not rush in blindly."

"Master." Gurax bowed his head again. "There is something you must know first."

"Speak," Saxüru allowed.

"I have sensed another in recent memory. While in our native realm or in this world I cannot say, since I did not even notice the breach." Gurax placed his arms across his chest, webbed fingers splayed, and palms pressed to his shoulders. "There is no excuse for that lapse. I accept whatever penance you decide."

"Later." Saxüru waved a hand dismissively. "Tell me now what I must know."

Gurax dropped arms to his side, his great locks of olive brown seaweed swirling with the current. "I and two others of my kind noticed a fissure of cold light, a day's swim through the waters northeast." He pointed. "We felt a presence on the other side, caught a scent unlike any other, and then saw its pale eye peering through. It flung itself against the fissure but was too large to pass and the rocks would not yield. As I have said, I know not whether it is this world it threatens or our own. But it will certainly try to pass through."

Saxüru studied Gurax's countenance, knowing before his servant even spoke. "The great one?"

Gurax nodded. "I could not mistake *that* smell. It is the foul one who feasts on our kindred. Determined to again be free."

Saxüru ran a cloven paw across his skull, between his curved horns. "I see. This changes things a bit." He paused, to make a show of careful consideration. When he spoke again, it was to give the command which would put his plan in motion. "Engage the humans, lure them to me. I would finally see these weapons which first damaged the veil. Perhaps we can even learn to use them."

With a smile and a single nod, Gurax acknowledged the command and spun about. A tremor sent shockwaves through the water as his body undulated and sped away, leaving whirling currents in his wake.

Though the swift departure had no effect on him, Saxüru's nostrils flared. He had to be very careful not to betray his every intention. Although Gurax could sometimes be utterly oblivious, there was indeed no mistaking that smell. The great one, the giant fish known as Dendan, would soon be released. Though it fed on his fish-men, Saxüru intended to use it, even as he used them.

Later, when he had what he wanted, he could pick and choose which of his underlings lived and which would die. Like the humans, they would serve at his pleasure, live and die as he decreed.

John S. Worth

Chapter 7

August 10, 1990
JTF 13 outpost at Camp Lemonnier
1300 hours

Cassie was glad to discover there would be yet another Sailor on the team, almost as glad as she was when she'd arrived at Camp Lemonnier and found she wasn't the only woman. Then, to sweeten the deal even more, she found out they were picking up the other squid, some E-5 fresh out of leadership training, all the way north at the Suez Canal. It was a good sign the bigwigs at Intel and HQ had liked her plans. They were making it easier than it otherwise might have been.

Which was a welcome relief. Sometimes it seemed the only thing she really had going for her was rank. As a Navy Ensign, O-1, she was one of the highest-ranking members of the team, but even that had its drawbacks. Command wasn't hers to wield. She was there for research, to help ensure the success of their mission.

She stepped into the briefing room and took a seat with the others. At the front of the room stood Captain Harold 'Hank' Grimson, a 27-year-old Marine from Chicago. She'd met him about a year ago upon her assignment and was immediately impressed by his affable yet disciplined leadership. He was a young black man, lean and muscled everywhere, and able to put everyone around him at ease without compromising his leadership in the least. In fact, his crew had learned to trust him implicitly and would follow him into hell if necessary.

A few Marines arrived after Cassie and settled in. Once everyone was there, Captain Grimson started. "By now you've all heard the scuttlebutt, so let me confirm the rumors; we just received new orders." He turned to a map of the Red Sea, drawn upon a mounted section of Plexiglas, picked up a grease pencil and marked their position near the southern entrance. "We're going to take the *Scorpius* out to rendezvous with a conventional squadron due to come through the gate within the week."

The gate he referred to was the Gate of Tears, *Bab-el Mandeb* in Arabic. It was the strait connecting the Gulf of Aden to the Red Sea. He dashed a line from their camp to a point about a third of the way up the map. "We'll steam with them until they take position along the southern half of the sea. Then we're on our own until we reach the Suez Canal." He completed the dashed course indicating their Period of Intended Movement.

"Here's our PIM. As you can see, we'll keep away from the shore unless otherwise instructed, and then meet up with another squadron as it enters from the Mediterranean." He marked another X at the north end. "That's when we'll pick up our newest member, Petty Officer Thomas McCraith. He's an E-5, Intelligence

Specialist 2nd Class. Ensign Straub will now fill us in on other details."

Cassie stood and walked up as Grimson took a seat. "Thank you, Captain," she said as she turned to face the room. "Most of you know about my work with intelligence. Here's what you might not know. The reason for our assignment is a request I made following retrieval of data from one of my probes. On our way to pick up Petty Officer McCraith, we'll deploy the probe midway, so it can investigate the anomaly I discovered."

She took a small staff and a remote from a nearby table. The staff was about three feet long with a small hook screwed to one end. She used it to reach up and grab the D-ring of a media screen. Pulling it down, she covered the Plexiglas map.

"Here are some stills taken from my data." She keyed the remote, activating the slide projector as Hank turned out the lights. The first image was cast onto the screen and a sense of gravity filled the room. "Here's what the data shows and what we intend to do…"

John S. Worth

Chapter 8

September 15, 1990
Entering the Red Sea via the Suez Canal
0450 hours

Red was keenly aware of the situation. He was little more than cargo, an unwanted addition that had better *not* become a distraction—and definitely not part of the crew. Still, he had been happy to berth with the Boatswain's Mates in the belly of the guided missile cruiser. Even if they were careful not to say much to him, he enjoyed the camaraderie they had with one another. It was a vicarious echo of the time spent on his destroyer, which already seemed long ago.

They'd crossed the ocean on short notice, leaving mid-August and steaming with other warships. The newly promoted Intelligence Specialist, 2nd Class Petty Officer McCraith, was fortunate to have caught this last-minute ride. Having just entered the Red Sea via the Suez Canal, the ship would soon take position, but first a short delay while Red quietly disembarked. The Cruiser met the smaller vessel before sunrise and slowed to a crawl.

As he threw his canvas rucksack over his shoulder, Red was careful not to wake the other sailors. Reveille had yet to sound, and he would leave without saying goodbye. Not that it mattered. There was no one to really say goodbye to. Proof of how isolated he'd been.

He stepped carefully up the ladder then slowly worked the long handle to open the door. Still moving quietly as possible, he pushed it open, stepped through, then dogged the door tightly behind. He followed the passageway toward a series of ladders, doors, and hatches that led to the aft deck.

As he worked his way topside, Red thought back on the past month. Given menial tasks, he was kept busy and out of the way. It did bother him, he supposed, that he was barely talked to, the men having been cautioned against trading info with this hitcher whose strange mission even the captain wasn't privy to.

That much was confirmed right after they'd left port, by the old man himself as he'd sent Red away from the all hands briefing. The master-at-arms had escorted Red away without a word. Just a shrug and a smile, then he sat with him in the chow hall until the brief was over.

They each poured a cup of coffee from the day's dregs and sat across from one another in the empty mess hall. Since he really had nothing to lose, Red decided to ply the master-at-arms for any answers he might have.

"Chief Jenkins," he started, adding sugar and stirring it in. "So, is this a top secret, need to know, all hands but me briefing? Or did I do something to piss the captain off?"

The man, an E-7 with just a bit of gray at his temples and a ridge for a brow, with sunken, brooding eyes, laced his hands and leaned back, cracking his knuckles. He sighed. "Kid, it ain't you. And I'm only saying this cause I figure, being part of 13, you know how to keep your mouth shut."

Red let the surprise show on his face. "You know about the Task Force?"

"Enough," Jenkins said, reaching for his cup. "Truth is the old man is lucky to have this command, *any* command. But it's not where he saw himself at this point in his career."

"So what happened?" Red took a sip, tried not to wince but failed.

The chief grinned, then took a deep swig, completely black and bitter. As he set the cup down, he said, "About four years ago, Captain Sloan was on his way up, jockeying for one of the carriers." The man's eyebrows raised. "Would've made it too. But then one night we were steaming through the Bermuda Triangle..."

Red scrunched his face skeptically.

The chief shrugged. "Yeah, I know. Any sailor worth his salt'll tell ya there's nothing to that bunk. They're right of course… until there is." He leaned in, propping elbows on the table. "Been through there a hundred times myself and never saw squat. But that night something was different. Noticed it when I was on the bridge."

The man leaned away again, but less at ease this time. His mind seemed to wander back. "Moon was full, sliding in and out of the clouds. No stars, though. Just black sky and dark water. And a blanket of fog that drifted just above the waves, tracking with the ship like a shroud draped over her masts.

"I was down in my rack when the ship took a sharp port turn. The sea had been calm, but I learned long ago to use the straps if I had 'em. We rolled hard, but that strap caught me. I figured it was nothing, so I just decided to ignore it and drop on back to sleep.

"Then the captain got on the 1MC…" The chief pointed to the nearest speaker wired into the 1 Main Circuit, used to make announcements to the crew at large. "Middle of the night and he keyed that thing up, so you knew right away it was something serious. Anyway, he called for me to report to the bridge ASAP. I throw on my khakis, sidearm and cuffs, and hoof it up there. I come in through the starboard passage and no sooner am I on the bridge than the captain orders me to cuff the officer of the deck."

"What the hell?" whispered Red, caught up in the tale.

"Exactly what I was thinking." Jenkins nodded. "Unheard of. And the officer of the deck, he's no slouch. He's a young lieutenant, A-J squared away, by the book, as levelheaded as they come. But the captain is livid. He's screaming for me to cuff the guy, and the lieutenant is screaming right back that everybody saw it. Downright adamant about something right off the starboard bow. Swore we were on a collision course when he ordered us hard to port."

"So, what did you do?"

"Whaddaya think! I did my job. Cuffed that lieutenant and put him in the brig. Captain Sloan and I go way back, was him helped get me this anchor on my collar. No way was I gonna betray that. We made a bee line for Norfolk, and then when we tie up to the pier… well it's then we notice the hull, right above the waterline on the starboard side.

"There's this weird, discolored pattern. Like someone took a garden hose and sprayed concentrated acid in a random line across all that gray paint. All dripped looking, brown, even ate into the metal.

"Let me guess," offered Red. "That's when things got dicey."

Chief Jenkins nodded. "To say the least. The Naval Investigative Service got involved, since you had a captain saying one thing and a respected lieutenant saying the opposite. Captain Sloan was hoping for a quick court-martial that would shut the guy up, but that wasn't gonna happen." The man took another long drink, then paused as if collecting his thoughts.

"These NIS guys, they start questioning the crew. Especially the lookouts and the bridge crew. They take samples from the hull. Go so far as to confine everyone to the ship, cordon off the starboard side so the deck crew doesn't start grinding or sanding to repaint.

"They bring me in, have me sign some paperwork about confidentiality and, since I'm the master-at-arms with a certain amount of bull-headedness concerning my own duty and self-perceived authority, I start pushing back just enough to find out who they really are."

"Not NIS," ventured Red.

The man gave a wan smile. "Intel branch of some task force I'd never heard of. JTF13."

"So long story short, what happened?"

"We came to a compromise," the chief said. "Was the lieutenant's idea, of all things. He let the captain save face, said they should let him keep his command with the understanding that the 'arrogant asshole', his words, not mine, should listen to his officers and care more about his crew than his career. Then he showed the old man by example. Said he'd take a demotion, so the story could be put to rest, without any mention of what almost happened."

"What was it," Red wanted to know. "What did you almost crash into?"

The chief shook his head. "Some kinda Sea-Dragon. Almost as long as the ship. Like Nessie on steroids. I caught sight of it in the fog, right after I cuffed the lieutenant's hands behind his back and turned him toward the side entrance.

"The thing raised its head and spewed a stream of fire or venom, maybe both, straight up into the air." Jenkins gave a mild snort. "I ignored the hell outta that, along with the lieutenant's renewed objections, and just got us off the bridge."

"So, did they take the deal? Was he reassigned?"

The man grinned and finished off his coffee. "You could say that. Even so, the captain was still pissed. That kind of sacrifice for the greater good ain't always welcomed. Especially when the politics of career advancement are involved. And even though he took the fall, busted back to Jr. Grade, in the end that officer came out all right. Got recruited into 13 Intel, from what I heard.

"Took two lookouts and some of the bridge crew with him. Not sure if they were all recruited or maybe just reassigned to other duty stations. But they definitely weren't allowed to stay here." The chief fixed Red with those deep-set eyes and smiled. "Just remember, you didn't hear any of that from me. And I'll deny every word if you squeal."

Red finished his own coffee and waved a hand in agreement. "Of course," he said. "Just one question."

The man raised his brows for Red to continue.

"That lieutenant. What was his name?"

The chief relaxed. "Morrison. Helluva guy. Probably saved a lotta lives that night. But again, you didn't hear that from me."

The all hands meeting ended. Once the crew started milling about, the man stood and motioned for Red to be on his way. They never spoke again.

During his entire ride, the crew seemed anxious and excited. Iraq had invaded Kuwait, the impetus of their quick turnaround. They'd been off the Virginia coast, testing their Mk 7 AEGIS weapons systems, when the invasion occurred.

They quickly returned to homeport in Norfolk, where they took on supplies, as well as Red, then got underway again with a convoy of other ships. Clearly, something was about to go down. Of course, it didn't take a genius to guess what warships armed to the teeth and steaming for the middle east might mean.

This, combined with the questions surrounding Red, seemed to color every glance his way with an odd mixture of awe and suspicion. At first it rankled him that he'd been all but marked an outcast. But after his conversation with Chief Jenkins, he had a better take on it. The captain's distrust was misdirected of course but made its own kind of sense—sort of.

So, he forced the feelings of alienation down, rationalized with the knowledge it was probably best for him and the crew that neither knew what the other was doing. What none of the crew realized was Red truly didn't know much of anything. He'd been kept in the dark concerning the mission of this convoy of ships *and* that of the operatives he'd soon be joining.

Matter of fact, once he'd really thought about it, Red had to admit his frustration had little to do with any dismissive treatment. It was because he *still* had no clue what he'd be doing. Though he trusted his chain of command and understood the need for secrecy, he *hated* not knowing.

For a solid month he'd been aboard this vessel, but even before then, he was told to get ready and left to wonder what in the world he was in for. The words of his last instructor at Quantico came to mind; "Compartmentalize. Become like a damn machine." That's what the man said after an intense training exercise.

Less than a month had passed since Red completed that leadership training at Quantico. After which he'd balked at an accelerated path for work in intelligence. So, he got what he wanted and was sent back to the field, assured by the higher ups that, before further investment, Thomas McCraith would get all the field time one man could stand. He'd secretly rejoiced at that. They underestimated how much he loved the proverbial briar patch.

As for the mission itself, all he was told up front was that he'd be attempting something of utmost importance, something near impossible. He was more anxious than scared. And any trepidation Red felt was tempered by the thrill of being on the ocean again.

So it was that Thomas McCraith, now 2nd Class Petty Officer, completed his entrance to the Red Sea. He passed through an open hatch and kept moving. As he climbed the final ladder leading topside, he made a final push to set all those feelings aside, compartmentalize and focus on getting where he needed to be.

He laughed inwardly at himself. It all kept coming to mind and he kept pushing it down. Maybe that instructor was right, but for Red it didn't come easy. At least he was reaching the point where someone would be forced to fill him in.

Chapter 9

September 15, 1990
The north end of the Red Sea

Red stepped onto the weather deck at 0500 hours and dogged down the final door. Making for the small cluster of men port side of the fantail, he prepared to depart and join JTF 13 aboard a fast attack patrol boat. He called down to the marine captain on the deck of the patrol boat, a young black man who looked only a bit older than himself. "Permission to come aboard?"

"Permission granted," the marine yelled back. His uniform's sleeves had been rolled up, and his massive forearms hinted at the muscle beneath the rest of his outfit. Dark sunglasses hid his eyes, and he wore no cap, sporting a high and tight with perfect fades on each side.

Red climbed down the rope ladder, nothing in his hands, just the pack on his back stuffed with his belongings. On his way down he spied a female sailor, E-4, at the controls, maintaining course and speed to keep proper distance between the boat and ship. There wasn't much room on the deck. He was boarding just forward of the bridge on the smaller vessel's starboard side. Two more marines tended lines that kept the ladder secure on their end.

"Fresh meat!" said the marine captain.

"So I keep hearing," Red replied, planting his feet on the deck. The ladder was retrieved, while the marines released the lines which slipped through the chocks and back to the cruiser. The vessels began to steer away from each other.

Red saluted the captain, dropping it only after the captain dropped his. "Also heard y'all needed some help." As he steadied himself on a stanchion, Red noticed the empty swivel-mount bolted to its top. He spied another, same spot on the port side. "Makeshift gun mounts?" he asked.

"For our 50 cals," said the marine captain. "We've made a few modifications to our Lucky Lady. Suppose you could call most of 'em upgrades, but sometimes we have to scrounge for parts, when an original piece needs replacing."

Red looked around. "A Hydrofoil. Nice." He took note of the armament; two quad RGM-84 Harpoon missile launchers on the back and a Mk-75 62 caliber up front, what the crew would call a 3-inch gun—for the diameter of the shells it fired.

The marine grinned. "PHM-7. The *Scorpius*, our sweet Lady Luck. They were gonna christen her 'Libra' for the seventh constellation of the zodiac—you know, blindfolded gal with scales in her hand, dealing justice. But *Scorpius* just sounded cooler, I guess. Besides, the

Scorpio is a water element and associated with the scorpion, snake, and eagle." He shrugged. "If you buy into all that stuff."

"No offense, sir," Red ventured. "But you sound like a walking dictionary."

The captain gave a friendly scowl. "You can be jealous of my manliness, combat skills, and rugged good looks, but don't go hating 'cause I'm smarter than you." He put a hand to a bulkhead and looked at the ship with affection. "Another thing about our Lady Luck, you won't find any public records on her. Like everything else with 13, we keep our lips sealed. Make sure you understand that. Now come on." The man started walking without offering a handshake, though he did say, "I'm Captain Harold Grimson, but you can call me Hank. We keep it informal, unless we're in mixed company. And we all know you're Petty Officer Thomas McCraith. So is it Tom, or just your last name, or—"

"Call me Red," he answered.

"For the hair." Hank nodded. "Of course."

"Either that or my neck."

Hank smiled. "Red it is."

First stop was the bridge. "Listen up," said Hank, as they stepped through the door and Red dogged it behind. "Everybody welcome the newest member of our crew." He gestured toward Red. "This is IS2 Thomas McCraith."

He nodded. "Just call me Red."

Without waiting, Hank went on, "At the helm is our Quartermaster, Third Class Petty Officer Diana Reshivik."

The young woman at the helm kept her eyes ahead. "Shiv," she said. "Good to have another squid aboard. E-5, huh? Should have your sea legs by now."

"I do. Pleased to meet you and glad to be here."

"That's Lance Corporal Johnson by the charts," Hank continued. "Usually their stations are reversed."

The young marine looked up. "I'm teaching her to drive and she's letting me nav-o-gate."

"The hell you are," Shiv replied, a smile on her lips. "I taught *you* to drive. Taught you damn near everything you know about this vessel."

Johnson grinned. "That's Shiv for you. Modest to a fault."

Hank kept going, "And Slim's our resident grease monkey."

A young man, probably 21 or 22 at the most, wiped his brow with an already oil-smeared rag. "Airman First Class David Pickins," he said. "The only Air Force on this crew, only decent mechanic, and only by-the-grace-of-God Texan."

"That's like three strikes against you right there," said Shiv, shaking her head.

"A triple threat, you mean," said Slim. He was about five foot ten, muscled but rangy, what Red recognized as farm muscle.

"Here I sit," chimed Johnson, "—cheeks a-flexin', giving birth to another Texan."

Slim popped him on the arm with the grease rag. "Shut it, you inbred Okie." He pointed to Shiv without looking her way. "And she's from California, if that tells you anything."

Just then the door on the opposite side opened and a young female Ensign stepped through.

Red felt his breath catch. She was about five-foot-four with jet black hair and striking blue eyes, her skin flawless. He felt his mouth go dry.

She looked right at him and blinked as though not believing her eyes. "It's you," she said, clearly troubled.

Red struggled to find his voice. "Uh...I'm sorry, have we met?"

She frowned. "I mean what I'm *sensing* ... it's coming from you."

Hank cocked his head at Red, studying him now. He questioned the Ensign while keeping his eyes on Red.

"Thought I felt something too. Figured it was just the lingering after-effects of a 13 course at Quantico."

Red looked from one to the other. "I've obviously raised some hackles here. But, just so you know, it's been over a month since I've been in any kind of training."

Johnson made a show of sniffing in Red's direction. Then he shook his head. "Can't smell anything over Slim here." He looked to the Airman. "When's the last time you showered?"

"Right after I snuck out your mama's bedroom window."

"Pipe down," said Hank. "Sorry, Red. It's something supernatural. Some of us are more attuned to it than others. Ensign Straub especially so."

She approached him and put out a hand. "Pleased to meet you, Petty Officer McCraith." Finally, she smiled. "Whatever it is I'm sensing isn't overbearing. But it isn't residual either. Are you wearing a talisman or something?"

Then it occurred to Red. He pulled out his wallet. "Maybe this?"

Her eyes widened as she took a step back. "Where did you get that?"

"Hey," Hank interjected, "just what the hell did you bring aboard my boat?"

Red shrugged. "I killed a Yacumama off the coast of Panama. Stripped part of its hide and made a wallet. Kind of what we do where I come from."

"Preach it, brother," said Slim. "You got some city slickers and straight up Yankees on board. Good folks, mind you, but wouldn't know a trot-line from a limb hook."

Hank started shaking his head. "Seriously? Please Lord, not another one."

"All due respect, sir," said Slim. "But you ain't turned down any of that deer jerky my brother Ray sends every year."

Cassie furrowed her brow, but her countenance softened just a bit. "Be careful, McCraith. We don't want to draw unwanted attention. Granted, the emanation is subtle, but it's there."

"Red," he said. "It's what most folks call me."

She raised an eyebrow and put a hand on the door to leave. "McCraith will do," she said, with just the hint of a smile. "And you can call me Ensign Straub."

"Yes ma'am," he answered, nothing but respect in his tone, and his best poker face.

After she'd stepped out and dogged the door behind, Shiv spoke up, "Subtle, my ass." She grinned as she changed her pitch and volume to mimic Cassie. "The *emanation* is subtle..." She gave Red a coy glance. "...but *it's* there."

Hank elbowed him. "Careful. Fraternization and all. And besides, we all got to work together."

Red started to defend himself, "I don't ... I mean, I wasn't trying to..."

Johnson pushed in, "And you better hope Belfry doesn't find out."

Red frowned. "That her boyfriend?"

"He wishes." Shiv laughed, eyes still ahead as she steered.

"Come on," Hank said. "Let's get you settled and answer some of those questions you must have. The *legitimate* ones."

Chapter 10

September 15, 1990
The Red Sea
0515 hours

Once outside the bridge, Hank led them to a hatch that was secured open. It was barely wide enough to squeeze through. He pointed to a ladder leading straight down. "Bunk area is below decks, so let's get your things squared away." He gave a 'hand me' gesture for the rucksack and nodded for Red to precede him.

Red slipped his pack from his shoulders and handed it over. He squeezed through the hatch, went down the ladder, then caught the bag as the marine tossed it down.

"Thank you, sir." Red ran a hand across a bulkhead as the captain descended. "I noticed the Scorpius is armed for bear."

"That's the idea." Hank hopped the last few rungs and hit the lower deck with a clang. "Fast and deadly. Get inside coastal waters and do a destroyer's worth of damage without as much overhead."

Red nodded. "So, if memory serves, these run about 12 knots in cruise mode, 48 on the foils?"

It earned him a look of respect. "And you called me a walking dictionary. You've done your homework."

Hank gestured with arms spread wide. "Here's the deluxe suite." The room was small with hammocks stretched everywhere. "You can hang your bag on a free hook there."

Red walked over and put the rucksack on the hook. "Excuse my ignorance, but I thought these were all in Key West, to stop drug runners and such."

Hank snorted as he headed for the door. "Yeah, the Navy underutilizes these. Kept her sisters tangled up in red tape. No doubt some level of personal politics involved."

"Sounds about right," Red conceded. He followed the marine further into the boat.

"As for the homeport, we're based out of Camp Lemonnier," said Hank. "The Djibouti government lets us park there, as long as we keep to ourselves and do a few favors now and then. So we're oh, only about 1400 miles from home port. Now we *are* the only *Pegasus* class hydrofoil in these waters, which can draw attention. But any fool dumb enough to try and push us around or pirate this vessel will live to regret it." He shrugged and gave a sly smile. "Or not."

"Gotcha." Red tried not to sound impatient. "So who's filling me in on mission details?"

Hank motioned Red to keep up. "I am. Everybody else is busy, getting ready. Besides, I'm the squad leader. You eat yet?"

Red shook his head.

"I'll brief you over breakfast. C'mon."

In the small dining area, they sat down to trays of scrambled eggs and salt-cured ham, cups of joe on the side.

Hank began by giving him a printed roster of the crew. Red studied it in silence:

- Crew Manifest, USS Scorpius PHM-7, Pegasus Class Hydrofoil -

Captain Harold 'Hank' Grimson: O-3, Marines. Age 27, Illinois. CO/Squad Leader.

Ensign Cassandra 'Cassie' Straub: O-1, Navy. Age 24, Florida. Intelligence Officer.

Corporal Wayne 'Waymore' Mooreland: E-4, Army. Age 23, Tennessee.

3rd Class Petty Officer Diana 'Shiv' Reshivik: E-4, Navy. Age 22, Los Angeles.

Private First-Class Duncan 'Dunc' Grizzard: E-2, Marines. Age 19, Colorado.

Lance Corporal Scott 'Johnson' Johnson: E-3, Marines. Age 21, Oklahoma.

Airman First Class David 'Slim' Pickins: E-3, Air Force. Age 21, Texas.

Seaman Elliot 'Belfry' Batson: E-3, Navy. Age 20, Michigan.

3rd Class Petty Officer Marcus 'Doc' Zelten: E-4 Navy. Age 23, Connecticut, Hospital Corpsman (HM3).

Private First-Class Elizabeth "Lizzy" Fields: E-3, Army. Age 20, Wisconsin.

Lance Corporal Don "Too-Tall" Hall: E-4, Marines. Age 24, Arizona.

Corporal Alfred "Big Al" Hinson: E-3, Marines. Age 22, Idaho.

Since he didn't have a photographic memory, Red decided he'd just have to get to know his crewmates in the course of time. There were only twelve, so it shouldn't take long.

When he looked up, Hank said, "You're our lucky thirteen. A ship this size should have, at the very least, a complement of seventeen enlisted and two officers. Right now, counting you, we're still a fire team short. Fortunately, we can manage three rotating shifts, 8 hours on, 8 off, and 8 to sleep. Of course, those last two don't always work out, but that's to be expected."

"We're all young, right?" Red replied, parroting every old salt he'd ever heard. "I'm sure we can handle it, sir."

Hank gave a wry grin. "Speak for yourself. I'm feeling older by the day." He took a sip of coffee, then added, "You can probably guess what the guys on the conventional end are up to."

"Gonna push Hussein back to his side of the sandbox," Red answered, as he speared a chunk of eggs.

"Here's the skinny on that. This buildup is going to position our forces all across the Med, Persian Gulf, and Red Sea. That cruiser you just left is preparing for an all-out assault on Iraq, if it comes to that. Air strikes, boots on the ground, and as many Tomahawks as needed."

"I'll believe that when I see it," Red muttered.

Hank nodded. "Understandable. And maybe Hussein will blink. Pull back and avoid a bloodbath. But I doubt it. My guess is that the world is about to see the first combat use of the Tomahawk, with no pulled punches. Hell, we've even got subs ready to launch."

"If all that's true, then it should end fast." Red started in on his breakfast.

Hank did the same but kept talking. "It should. But we both know how these things can go. Could be over quick or be drawn out for years. Maybe even a little of both."

"Wish I could see one launch," Red said. "A Tomahawk, I mean."

Hank whispered conspiratorially, "I hear they'll be authorized to fire hundreds. Gonna target Iraqi military leaders, their electric grid, even their oil."

"Hope Saddam backs down," Red answered, his face in his plate. "If not, I hope we go all in and cut off the head. Put a decisive end to this mess." He looked up. "So where do we fit in with all of this?"

Hank arched his eyebrows. "13 has been clearing the way. Local rumors have it, the old Babylonian 'god', Saxüru, has been awakened. He's some kind of water deity with a lot of wicked creatures at his command."

That got Red's attention. "So, we're attacking a god."

Hank shook his head. "Slow your roll there, Red. First of all, I don't regard him as such. Just some beast from another dimension that's slipped through into ours." He sipped his coffee. "And like I said, 13 is putting out fires, keeping the path clear for the big guns. As for our *specific* assignment, let's just say it's completely off the wall. One of Cassie's crazy ideas that she managed to sell the brass on."

"Sir, you're killing me," Red groaned. "Start with the big picture if you want but get to our part. Are we supposed to *kill* this Saxüru creature?"

Hank smiled, finished eating his ham, then continued, "The bigger mission is a need-to-know basis. Matter of fact, except for the ones on this boat, only four others at HQ and Intelligence even know our destination. We've got a full squad on board, now that you're here. Like I said, we could use four more, but you use the team you're given. As for our mission, I'll cut to the chase: you're gonna be our primary swimmer. Heard you're like a cross between a fish and a pit bull."

"So, what am I swimming after?" Red finished off his eggs. "Need me to kill a Kraken or a Nymph? Any Mermaids in this region?"

Hank's face grew serious. "Better hope like hell we don't wake a Kraken. But you're closer than you think. There are merfolk in these waters, all the way from the Red Sea to the Persian Gulf. Though the locals don't call them that. And it isn't a mermaid we're after. It's a *merman*. Much more vicious. Very territorial."

Red raised an eyebrow and finished off his coffee. "So we're out here to kill mermen."

Captain Hank Grimson cocked his head. "Not quite. We only need one, and hopefully there won't be any killing."

"You heard about the North Sea, didn't you? What I did at *Piper Alpha*—"

"Of course, I was briefed on you. Told that if anyone could do this job, it was you. Our orders are to get one for the brainiacs at Intel to study. They want us to bring one in alive."

Chapter 11

September 18, 1990
Center of The Red Sea, about 100 miles offshore
between Sudan and Syria
1020 hours

Cassie, Red, and Hank stood on the aft deck of the Scorpius. Belfry was on the bow with two more marines posted outside either door of the bridge. All three were armed with M-16s. The rest manned their stations inside.

Cassie stared at the weights. Twenty-five pounds, fitted into a harness lashed across Red's shoulders. The extra weight would drop him faster, while the design allowed him to shed it quickly and ascend in seconds.

She shook her head in disbelief. "We must be out of our ever-loving minds. It's not too late to back out, McCraith. I'll take the heat, say it was my decision."

Red completed the check of his harness straps. "This is where your probe spotted them, right?" He picked up a dark, metallic staff, about thirty inches long with opposing prongs at one end.

"And as I said during the brief, that doesn't mean any of them are here now. But yeah, this is our best bet."

"Our fish finder shows two objects," Hank said, a tending line in hand. He had a headset in place, relaying info from the lower deck. "They're the right size but could just be sharks." He shook his head. "I gotta say, that's some of the most Jerry-rigged 'sonar' I've ever seen." Checking the clasp a final time, he said, "Belfry's got the chum bucket ready. Sure you wanna go that route?"

Red sighed. "Captain, we planned this out best we can. So, all due respect, let's just stop this second guessing." He pulled the goggles over his eyes. "We want this sonofabitch alive; we better embrace a little crazy." He looked back at Hank. "Tell Belfry to chum the waters."

Hank clipped the tether to the back of Red's harness, then keyed his mic. "Baitcaster to Bucketman, Operation Dagon is a go."

He paused as he listened to the reply over his headphones, smiled at Red, then keyed his mic a second time. "Roger that, chum's away."

They waited. Cassie gave a slow visual sweep of the surface. "What if they don't like our seafood platter?"

Red stepped to the edge. "Don't worry. I added my secret sauce."

Cassie frowned. "Should I be concerned?"

Red showed them his palm. A fresh incision marked it. "These things have a taste for human flesh, so I added a few drops of my blood to whet their appetite."

Without waiting for another word, he stepped off the side.

As soon as he went under, Red reached back and deftly unclipped the tether. He needed as much freedom of movement as possible and would deal with any repercussions later. If they were gonna hand him an impossible job, then to hell with protocol.

The harness would weigh him down, but his arms could still move freely. He focused on that and took a few test swings. If the males were more aggressive than that female he'd fought before, he'd need to strike first and hit hard. He had a better idea than any of the others what he'd be up against, and he'd prepared accordingly.

The short staff in his hands was more than a prod. He'd already modified the internals. The voltage would step up high enough to knock out a Great White. He studied the dark waters intently as the weights continued to pull him down.

"Damn it, Red!" Hank yelled as he noticed the line go slack. He reeled it in. Just as he thought, there was no damage. Just an empty clasp on the end.

"What the hell!" exclaimed Cassie. "I thought you secured that!"

"I did! Damn moron undid it."

"Why would he do that?"

"How should I know? I just met the stupid bastard." Hank keyed his mic; "Everyone keep an eye out. McCraith's off his leash and probably gonna get himself killed. Gunners, don't fire unless I give the order."

The first thing Red saw was an ugly grimace coming up at him. Slow and deliberate, the thing put on a show, shaking its scaled head in a menacing display, clearly meant to seize its prey's attention and paralyze with fear. The creature clawed its way up from the brine, snapping its wide jaws to expose rows of crowded teeth. A mane of seaweed writhed, like a nest of vipers, about its angular skull. It reminded Red of the creature he'd seen near Scotland, though this one was much larger and more muscular. Definitely male.

The young sailor kicked his way deeper, closing the gap. A plan had quickly formed, as he remembered what his training had taught him. Such a brazen display by the merman was calculated. His suspicion aroused, Red shoved the prod behind him as he descended.

Just as he'd suspected, a second creature had flanked. The prod struck flesh and Red hit the switch, sending a jolt into his unseen assailant. The first creature shrieked, its face contorting into an angry snarl as it hastened its ascent.

Without looking behind him, Red whipped the prod back around, just as a pair of claws reached up. Before Red could strike, the creature grabbed his wrist, making it impossible for him to use the weapon. The sailor improvised. With his other hand he executed a quick jab, tagging the monster right between the eyes on the bridge of its stubbed nose.

The water clouded with a small plume of blood, which instantly obscured the merman's gaping mouth. The thing's grip also loosened, just enough for Red to wrest his hand free. Wasting no time, he flicked the prod forward and zapped the creature right in its grimacing face.

It went limp and fell into blackness.

Red let it go. Popping a set of weights free, he kicked, reversing his course. On his way up, he reached out, snagging the other stunned merman by the wrist.

Red slid the prod into its sheath on his side and dropped another ten pounds. He kicked again, dragging the creature up with him.

As Red broke the surface, Hank grabbed the tether again. He locked eyes with Red, shouted "Heads up!" then tossed it.

Keeping one arm clamped around the creature's neck, Red snagged the line, mere inches from the metal clasp. Wasting no time, Hank reeled them back to the *Scorpius* where two marines slipped shepherd hooks through Red's harness. Quickly they hauled him over the side.

Once aboard, Red dropped the merman to the deck. Cassie moved in, handcuffs at the ready. She whipped one cuff across a scaled wrist, locked it down tight, and proceeded to flip the creature.

Its eyes shot open and it lashed out, raking with its free claw. Cassie jumped back, as talons ripped across her forearm. In her periphery, she saw a weapon brought to bear. "Put that away!" A shot rang out. "No!" she yelled at the marine, "We need it alive!"

The creature pushed up with one arm. Cassie looked down in surprise as it snagged her ankle, tripping her to the deck. She kicked free and backed away on elbows as it clawed for her.

Red brought his staff into play. Shoving it to the thing's chest, he delivered another jolt. The merman fell limp.

Cassie turned on her side, to face the young marine, fixing him with an icy gaze. "Johnson, you'd better have a damn good reason for firing that sidearm."

The marine pointed behind her with his free hand as he holstered the pistol.

Cassie pushed herself into a seated position and turned to discover what everyone else had seen. On the deck behind her, half its tail dangling over the side, was another merman. A single hole marked the center of its forehead. Its eyes were open, but vacant. Its bearded face lay slack-jawed in a puddle of blood.

"Get a med-kit over here!" shouted Red. He nodded to Cassie. "Best disinfect and dress that wound."

She frowned, with a sideways glance at the corpse. "Pretty sure that one's a goner."

"For your arm." Red laughed as he started to holster the prod. "And yeah, it's too late for Flipper."

Cassie got to her feet. She finally noticed the long, bloody slits along her right arm. Which she promptly ignored.

Hank turned the stunned man-fish on its belly, to finish cuffing the claws behind its back. "Keep that staff at the ready," he said, which put the brakes on Red. "Seems to me they recover fast. Johnson and Waymore, help me get this thing below."

"What about the dead one?" asked Johnson, as he bent to help Hank.

"Put it on ice," said Cassie, as their Hospital Corpsman, HM3 Marcus Zelten, opened his med-kit and set to work. "Intel can dissect it if they want. Study a living and dead specimen."

"Hell," said Belfry, stepping close enough to join in. "We might all get promoted." He knelt to the corpse and dragged its tail onto the deck. "Ain't every day the brainiacs have their cake and eat it, too."

Johnson raised his eyebrows and grinned. "Crab cake and Sushi." He glanced at the dead one. "Think they'll notice if we take a thin filet? Or two?"

"Enough jawing," said Hank. "Let's get crab-cake here to the tank." Waymore grabbed the stunned merman around the waist. Hank had the head and chest, while Johnson hefted the legs. They started for the nearest stairwell. Red kicked off his flippers and picked them up. He took position behind the unconscious beast, prod at the ready just in case it was needed again.

Belfry and two others hefted the dead one onto a tarp. Cinched it up on either end so they could get it to the cooler. They all moved to the stairwell to heft their catch below decks.

Once Red and the others were gone, Cassie grew silent. She stood quietly on the deck, lost in thought while 'Doc', as Zelten was called, treated her cuts. As he dressed her wounds with sterile gauze, she ran through events again in her mind.

She couldn't help but be bothered by Red's behavior. The others may have forgotten, but she couldn't ignore the way he'd strayed from their plan. How he'd jumped in the water untethered, with no warning and, afterward, no apparent remorse.

Sure, it had all ended well. She looked at her slashed arm. Okay, reasonably well. She shook her head. Those were minor flesh wounds, and she knew it. Hell, if she was being honest, it had ended great. Two specimens!

Then again, did the ends justify the means? That was the real question, and a slippery damn slope. What if it hadn't ended well? What if he'd gotten himself killed? Or someone else? Why had he done it, anyway? Was it a death wish? Or some macho Rambo crap? Whatever the reason, it couldn't be ignored.

She would mention it during their debrief, but she would also include it in her report. And even if they all ended up hating her for it, Cassie's mind was made up. She had a job to do, after all. They all did. And it mattered how they did it. She sighed and looked out over the sea.

"Damn you, McCraith." She shook her head. Regardless of Belfry's quip, she was pretty sure all-around promotions were not in the cards.

John S. Worth

Chapter 12

September 18, 1990
Steaming south along The Red Sea
1220 hours

With the live one secured and guarded, the *Scorpius* got underway. A cargo plane would meet them at Lemonnier and transport the creatures to Quantico.

Within a few hours, pertinent team members met to debrief. Seated on the berthing floor, in a rough circle, each member went over events, giving a rundown of their own activities and assessment of mission objectives. All in all, the consensus was an overwhelming success. Until it got to Cassie.

"While the mission results are undeniable, I have to point out two glaring deviations." She paused, taking no pleasure in what she had to say. "First when Petty Officer McCraith bled into the chum, and again when he removed his tether."

"Agreed," Red admitted, taking them all by surprise. "I strayed from the plan. Made a tactical decision in the moment and acted accordingly."

Cassie kept her voice neutral, "And now you need to explain those actions."

Johnson spoke up, "All due respect, Lieutenant—"

"No," Hank interrupted, "she's right. Go ahead, Petty Officer McCraith, let's hear your reasoning for that tactical decision."

Red swallowed hard, taken aback by the sudden shift to formality. "I've faced these things before. Knew they had a taste for human flesh, so I made sure the chum would do its job. As for the tether, as soon as you clipped it on, I felt it. Then I stepped off and made a split-second decision. Didn't want to risk any drag on my descent, so I unclipped it. Besides, those things can bite right through a line."

"There's some glaring inconsistency in your statements," Hank pressed, "beginning with a third deviation both you and Ensign Straub have overlooked." This earned him puzzled looks all around. "When you left the deck and entered the water. You didn't wait for us to give you the go ahead. Didn't signal your intentions, just dropped over the side."

Red nodded. "Guess I got caught up in the moment. I knew there were two contacts down there. Wanted to engage before they got away."

Hank shook his head. "That isn't it. Oh, I believe you *think* that's the reason, but you're wrong."

Trying not to sound defensive, Red asked, "What am I missing here?"

Hank dropped the formality. "Red, we've all had to adapt in the moment. Hell, we jettison entire plans midstream due to crazy shit nobody saw coming. Survival depends on being able to improvise and overcome." He sighed. "But there were no emergent threats in this scenario. Nothing unanticipated. Until your willful, split-second decisions to needlessly go off script. And you need to realize that for yourself. Just like we all do." He looked around at each team member. "We were all so hyped by exceeding the mission goals that we let confidence turn into cockiness. Good thing we had Ensign Straub to set us straight." He turned to her. "Good job, Ensign, and thank you."

She gave a solemn nod, taking no satisfaction in the compliment.

Red spoke up again. "I'm truly sorry. And if I'm wrong, I'm wrong. But I've learned to trust my gut. My instincts were kicking in, so I rolled with them. Didn't mean to put the mission or any of you at risk."

"I'm calling bullshit again," said Hank, his voice thick with exasperation. "You had time to run every decision by the team, yet you chose not to, whether consciously or not. Now stop this lame ass tap dance and tell us why."

Red took a moment, collecting his thoughts and his nerves. "I've learned to trust my guts, my instincts—but I guess I haven't learned to trust the men and women around me. And, though I didn't think of it this way at the time, I reckon I didn't run my ideas by the team because I didn't want to risk hearing *no*."

"Ask forgiveness, not permission. That it?" asked Hank.

With remorse in his eyes Red met the marine captain's gaze. "Yeah, I reckon so."

Cassie finally pressed in, hoping to bring things to a close. "McCraith, you can trust us. And we need to know we can trust you. That's really all this amounts to."

"And any bullshit," added Hank, "like trust issues, problems with authority, all that has to go. So, are you ready to move past it, or is this gonna happen again?"

"It won't happen again." Red looked to Cassie. "And thank you, Ensign. I mean that. Seems I got a huge stinking blind spot that nobody, but you were willing to point out."

Cassie gave an uncertain smile. "You know it still goes in the official report."

"Which I completely understand and agree with."

Hank checked his wristwatch. "Let's close this out, before I get all teary-eyed and we end up singing Kumbaya."

"I got a ukulele," said Belfry. "She's missing a string, but we can fake our way through."

Hank smiled. "End of brief." He got to his feet, as the others did the same.

"Lame ass tap dance," said Belfry, laughing. "That's a good one. Make a great song title."

Hank tried not to laugh as he opened the door. "Dismissed."

Chapter 13

September 20, 1990
Camp Lemonnier, Djibouti
1215 hours

Back at the camp, Hank and Cassie gave Red the grand tour.

"Lemonnier ain't exactly the Hilton," Hank said as he pointed to the ramshackle buildings. "Local politics being what they are, we're lucky to even be here. Truth is the Djibouti government is in a state of flux. It's—"

"A mess is what it is," Cassie cut in. "Civil war and unrest combined with shifting alliances by our own government. So, I'm not sure I'd call us lucky. More than a little dangerous for us, for everyone really. Still, it's strategically placed so we made an offer in return for our covert presence."

"Let me guess." Red rubbed his chin thoughtfully. "Keep the boogeymen away and we can park the *Scorpius*, camp in the outhouse, and store our supplies."

Hank nodded. "All very controlled, of course. Which is why we run on a shoestring and can't say boo without their permission."

"Place looks like a dump. Seriously, this is the best JTF can do?"

"For now," said Cassie. "But give it time. If things go our way Lemonnier could become much more than what it is now."

"Would've liked to have seen it in its heyday." Hank brushed a ragged stone wall with his fingertips. "She was established by the French Foreign Legion, you know."

"Didn't," replied Red. "But the cool factor just rose exponentially."

Cassie's tone grew somber. "There's the cargo plane."

The plane was a UC-12B Huron, modified by the Navy with an additional cargo door. It travelled with a small crew; a pilot, co-pilot, two marines, and a familiar face. Two silver bars marked his rank advancement to full lieutenant. As he approached alone, Cassie, Hank, and Red gave the requisite salute.

Lieutenant Morrison returned their salutes, then nodded to Red. "Hear you're handing us more than we asked for."

"Good to see you again, Lieutenant," Red replied, dropping into parade rest.

The man gave the slightest of smiles. "At ease, Petty Officer McCraith."

Red brought his hands back around, hooked a thumb in his pocket and propped the other wrist on his .45.

The lieutenant studied Red with an uncertain expression, as if he was searching for something. Finally, he looked to Hank and said, "You know the fleet is moving to the 9mm. Entire U.S. Military, in fact. I can probably get you up to speed?"

Hank shook his head. "I like the .45. Ain't broke and all that. But thanks anyway, sir. I do appreciate the offer."

Morrison shrugged. "Okay, but if you change your mind..." He looked back to Red, sighed, and then started again, "Petty Officer McCraith, normally I'd deliver this spiel privately, but since your team members here have already advocated, I'll keep them in the loop."

He acknowledged each with a glance, then spoke directly again to Red, "Petty Officer, we read the report as soon as it was transmitted. Long story short, while we're pleased with the outcome, the only reason you're keeping all your stripes is because these two convinced us you should." His eyes narrowed. "Don't make us regret that decision."

"Thank you, sir." Red let out a breath of relief.

Morrison nodded then addressed Cassie, "Ensign, you ready to go?"

"Just have to get my bags." She craned her neck to look at his crew. "So, which one's my replacement?"

Morrison raised an eyebrow. "McCraith is your replacement."

Hank spoke up, "Lieutenant, what the hell? I knew Cassie was up for reassignment, but her work here is—"

"In good hands," Morrison finished for him. He clasped Red by a shoulder. "McCraith is more than just some gung-ho SEAL washout. He can pick up right where Straub left off. Besides, it was her idea to capture the creature. We want her to drive point on the Intel. C'mon Straub, let's get moving." He turned before anyone could utter a word and made his way back toward the plane.

Hank yelled after him, "Hey! Instead of those 9mms, how about just an entire crew for once?"

Morrison kept walking, pretending not to hear.

"Let it go, Hank," Cassie said, putting a hand on his elbow. "Just do me a favor and get the crew together. I want to get a picture of everyone in front of the *Scorpius*."

While she hurried away to get her camera, Hank mustered everyone he could in front of the ship. Only a few were missing. "You too, Red," he said, as Cassie came jogging back.

"Where's Belfry, Waymore, and Shiv?" Cassie asked.

"At the barracks," said Hank. "Belfry was on the can and the other two ... uh ... indisposed, I guess is the best way to put it."

She frowned. She was running out of time and couldn't actually wait for them. "Well, I've still got to pack my stuff so maybe I'll see them."

"Yeah, let's get this done," said Hank. He hoped she didn't take it the wrong way, but chances were she knew by now he hated goodbyes and really just wanted this one behind him. "Johnson, Dunc, you knuckleheads stand next to me." As they moved in on either side, Hank took each under an arm, grinning while he pulled them close — almost in headlocks. Cassie took a few pictures, then smiled.

Red stepped away from the group, toward her. "Let me take a few with you in it. You'll want to have that."

She smiled and handed him the camera. "Thank you."

Once she'd settled in next to Slim and Doc, Red snapped two photos. "Perfect."

Cassie looked around sadly. "I gotta get going now."

"Not without a better goodbye," said Slim. "Come in for a big Texas hug."

She obliged him with a smile, then made it through a series of hugs and handshakes with only a few tears shed. One by one, they all drifted away.

She offered a hand to Red. "See you around, McCraith."

He shook it, then passed the camera to her. "Thanks again, Ensign."

"Call me Cassie, all right? Unless we're in mixed company, or for protocol."

"Sure thing, Cassie." He propped his hand back on his sidearm.

She smiled. "Wish we could've gotten to know each other better."

"My loss, but I'm an IS by rating. High chance our paths might cross again."

She turned to Hank. "Thanks for putting up with me."

They hugged as he said, "Whatever. You keep those eggheads straight and see if you can find out what the hell is going on."

When they separated, she nodded. "Yeah, and I'll be sure to slip all that 'need to know' Intel right your way."

"Take care of yourself, Cassie."

She nodded. "You, too. I'm gonna go get my gear and tell the rest of the team goodbye. *If* I can find them."

"Just try not to make Belfry cry. You know he's sweet on you."

She made a face. "Don't say crazy crap like that. Hell, sea monsters and djinn are bad enough." She hurried away, shaking her head.

When she was out of earshot Hank said, "It's the truth, and he probably is gonna cry."

Red ventured, "So, you knew that was coming?"

Hank ran a hand across his chin. "We all did. But I figured we might finally get staffed up proper. Now we stay right below just *enough*." He looked at Red. "Gotta tell you, she set a high bar. Hope Morrison is right about you." Without another word he turned to go.

Red turned his attention to the landing strip beyond their barracks, where the plane crew was loading a huge ice chest and the prison aquarium. He muttered to himself, "You and me both."

Part Two: Red Sea Rising

John S. Worth

Chapter 14

September 22, 1990
Marine Corps Base Quantico, Virginia
0400 hours

After a thirty-hour flight, with two stops and one in-flight refuel, the plane reached Quantico at 4 AM Eastern Time. In her new on-base apartment, Cassie opened her bags and began putting things in their places. She brushed her teeth, washed her face, and prepared to start shifting her sleep pattern. She'd managed to catch most of her hours on the flight and would try a few more before reporting for duty. Then, just as she was getting to bed, she decided to tend her wound.

Cassie unwrapped her bandaged arm to apply fresh antibiotic and a clean dressing. She gasped in shock as she removed the gauze. She'd uncovered a mass of cracked, blackened skin. There was no pain, no smell of decay, just a severely damaged forearm.

The cuts where the merman slashed had widened, the flesh inside looked dark and dry. Pustules had formed from wrist to elbow. Strangest of all, though her arm was a glaring wound, there was absolutely no pain.

She noted too that her hand remained unaffected; fingers fully mobile, with tactile sensation in her fingertips and even on the back of her hand as she stroked it with the other. It was the damndest thing. She redressed the wound, contacted her chain of command, and was promptly directed to the Task Force medic.

Within minutes she had driven herself to the infirmary, where she met with Dr. Imelda Conte. Cassie spent the next hour being questioned, examined, tested, x-rayed, and scanned. She gave saliva, urine, and blood samples. The wound was swabbed, probed, and photographed. She received heavy doses of antibiotics, injected right into the arm.

Before three hours passed, Dr. Conte gave her assessment. "We'll have to take the arm."

"But it doesn't even hurt," Cassie protested, "And my hand is completely fine. Can't you just cut out the bad parts or something."

The doctor frowned. "It's slow moving, which is all that's saving you. But it is spreading. Hasn't reached the bone yet, but it's close. No known meds are going to stop it. We'll save as much of the arm as we can, but we can't save the hand. By this time tomorrow it will reach your fingers and move higher up your arm. Unless it reaches bone first."

"And if that happens…?"

"My guess is that your arm will snap off and it will keep crawling its way up until you are dead."

"You're sure there's no other way."

"Not this time, Ensign. I'm so sorry." She said it again, "We have to amputate...before it's too late."

Though not exactly a death sentence, the doctor's prognosis was an unexpected blow. For Ensign Cassandra Straub, things would never be the same. She wondered if she'd ever be allowed back in the field. Then her determination kicked in and she decided that whatever happened, she'd do what she must and keep pushing for what she wanted. Like she always had.

She looked at the doctor and set her jaw. "Then I guess we'd better get this done."

Hardly a month later, Cassie stood before the saltwater tank, facing the creature.

"Can't get anywhere with our marine biologist or even our cryptozoologist," Morrison said. "I know you're still healing, but—"

She put up her left hand. "I'm fine," said Cassie. "And I called you first, remember? Besides, I've got an idea."

Morrison noticed the folder tucked under her right arm, which now ended at the elbow. "What exactly?"

She smirked. "Flash cards."

His brow furrowed. "Seriously?"

She reached and took the folder with her good hand. "You're trying too hard. Too high tech for your own good." She handed him the folder, and he looked inside.

Morrison gave a slow, appreciative nod. "Should've gotten your input sooner."

"It's okay." She took the folder as he handed it back. "It was my research that got him here. Shoulda known I'd have to champion this puppy to the end. Or mudpuppy, or whatever the hell he is."

Morrison laughed. "Call me if you need anything." He made a show of snapping his fingers, as if remembering. "Oh yeah, just so you know…" He tapped the insignia on his own collar. "You're out of uniform, *Lieutenant Junior Grade*." He turned and walked away.

Cassie yelled after him, "Thank you, sir!"

He didn't look, but shouted back, "Congratulations, Straub. I'll expect a report in the morning."

During the very first minute of the session, Cassie showed the creature a photo of an ancient Sumerian carving. She was immediately rewarded.

The creature thumped his chest and jerked his chin up, rising in the tank to spread fins and tail wide in a prideful display. He also began to chatter, interspersing the unintelligible clicks and chirps with what was obviously an ancient human language.

Within the hour, a linguist was called in, who was able to parse a few words, including the ancient name of Dagon, which was pronounced a bit differently from the Anglicized version. It seemed their operation to capture a live fish-man was aptly named.

Before the session ended, they'd parsed the creature's name: *Gurax.* He claimed to be a scion of Dagon. Whether or not he was the actual offspring of a mythical god, Cassie didn't know, but she put it all in the report for Morrison the next day. Then she scoured every source she could find on the deity.

She also collected more ancient images to begin a rudimentary form of communication. After several sessions with Gurax and the linguist, a dialogue finally became possible.

Chapter 15

December 15, 1990
Palms Memorial Cemetery
Kerrsville Georgia
1300 hours

With two marines and another sailor, Red lifted the coffin, then followed the chaplain who led them from hearse to gravesite. Red had spent the past few days answering to Tom or Tommy, finding small comforts in that and the familiar trappings of home. Then, earlier in the day, he'd met with the other servicemen to go over the order of events. Of course it wasn't how he'd pictured the holiday season. But, if not for the funeral, he wondered if he would've even taken leave or come stateside at all.

Pushing the thought away, he focused on the moment and found himself thankful for the efforts so many had made to get him here. This reconnection with his parents was long overdue. And the honor of laying to rest and paying his final respects to his grandfather, Jack McCraith, was a sacred privilege.

They set the coffin over the grave, ensuring the flag was securely in place as the chaplain motioned for the family to be seated. Red would not be sitting. He'd asked and was allowed to participate in the ceremony, so he moved to one side with the casket team, as the chaplain began the eulogy and sermon.

Red discretely watched his dad, Donald McCraith, who sat in the front row, being comforted by the woman who had shared his life and borne their only son. Lucinda held her husband's hand, leaned her head against his shoulder, and smiled over at her son. She mouthed the words, "So handsome."

Red gave a slight smile, then focused on the service. The chaplain kept it short and respectful, mentioning the sacrifice and dedication of men like Jack McCraith. He hit the high points of Jack's enlistment followed by life achievements after the Second World War ended. He closed by reading Psalms 23 and asked the family to rise for the 21-gun salute. Like the other service members Red held a salute during the rifle volleys and throughout the playing of Taps.

As the chaplain once more asked the family to be seated, Thomas McCraith stepped up for the final honor. He took one end of the flag as a marine took the other. They folded it until nothing showed but a triangle of blue with white stars. Here protocol was altered, as the marine stepped quietly aside and Red turned to face his father. He marched over and knelt to present the flag to his daddy.

With a lump in his throat Red somehow managed the words; "On behalf of the President of the United States, the United States Marine Corps, and a grateful nation, please accept this flag as a symbol of appreciation for *our* loved one's honorable and faithful service."

Donald McCraith couldn't speak. But with tears on his cheeks, he took the flag and smiled at his son. Red stood and saluted his father, which completely undid the man. Sobbing, Donald stood, returned the salute, then the two embraced. When they parted, Don found his voice, "Thank you, Tommy. That was beautiful."

Red gave a short nod, turned and saluted the casket. He held the salute and was joined by everyone in uniform, many veterans who were not, and others who stood and put their hands over their hearts, while the casket was lowered into the ground. Finally, the chaplain dismissed everyone, and the ceremony ended. With his service to this world over at last, Jack McCraith was finally and forever at peace.

The afternoon was a mixture of starts and stops as time alternately crawled and rushed amid the mourning during the ceremony, then visiting relatives who hadn't seen each other in years. There was laughter, a few tears, stories about his grandfather, old photo albums, then shared memories, and food. So much food.

When the day finally ended, Red drove his grandfather's old '69 Chevy pickup, following his parents to a home that was no longer his, in the truck his dad inherited but didn't really need.

The next morning, he woke to the smell of bacon. Wasting little time, Red showered, shaved, and dressed, then joined his folks in their small kitchen.

He kissed his mama, poured himself coffee, and sat across from his daddy. "You holding up alright?" he asked.

His old man nodded. "Your papa lived a full life. I'd like to have had another ten years with him but…You know." He shrugged, then pulled an envelope from his shirt pocket. "He wanted you to have this."

Red waited for his dad to set it down and pull his hand away before reaching. He didn't want to give the impression he was eager for inheritance or whatever it happened to be. His fingers settled on the small envelope.

"Open it," his dad said, a smile playing at his lips.

Red did, just as his mother put a plate of bacon and eggs on the table. The first thing he noticed was the Purple Heart. There was a photo lodged inside as well, almost the size of the envelope. Red took out the medal and held it almost reverently. "Daddy, you take this medal. What am I going to do with it?"

His dad put up a hand. "You're the one defending our country now. Besides, maybe that'll help you keep going when things get tough. And remind you of the price paid by those who went before."

Red stared, unsure if the man was needlessly putting salt in a wound. Finally, he said softly, "I didn't quit because things got tough. You might not believe that, but it's true."

Confusion clouded his dad's face. "I wasn't saying you did." Then he must have realized how he'd come across and shook his head vigorously. "Naw, no, hell no. That's not what I meant at all." He sighed. "Son, I don't care that you rang that bell. Nothing wrong with being a SEAL, but nothing wrong with not being one, either."

Uncertain, Red decided to give him the benefit of the doubt. "Sorry, thought I was over all that, but guess I'm still a bit...*defensive*." He put the medal in his shirt pocket and went back to the envelope.

"Is that what I think it is?" asked his mama, craning her neck as she sat by her husband.

Donald grinned. "It is."

She shook her head and started spreading jam on a biscuit. "Well, I just hope you're right then."

Red paused. "Right about what?"

"About you." Donald sipped his coffee and turned to face his wife. "Lucinda, this breakfast smells and looks delicious. And for once you're gonna see. I am right."

Donald took a biscuit, then looked back to his son. "Dang it, Tommy, take it out of that envelope already."

With an exaggerated wide-eyed expression, Red answered, "Okaaaay." Gingerly, he fetched out the tattered black and white photo. There was his grandfather, kneeling with a rifle in his hand and a group of young soldiers around him. He looked to be about the same age as Red was now.

But it was the bottom edge of the photo that caught Red's attention. There, stretched out at the feet of the young marines was a massive reptile. It looked like a Pteranodon, but with forelimbs that were definitely *not* attached to its wings. The thing had a pair of tusks jutting from either side of its lower jaw and about eight spikes crowning its head. "A dragon," Red whispered.

"Your grandpa and I sensed the supernatural on that rubbing you brought back from Scotland." The paper was currently pressed flat behind glass, hanging in the now abandoned house across the street, in his grandfather's old study.

His dad went on, "Then I felt it when you stopped in after that row with Noriega. Makes the hair stand up on my neck even now." He squinted at his son, as if searching for something in the young man's soul. "What am I sensing, Tommy?"

Red's head was reeling from it all. "Not sure I..."

"You've got the air of something supernatural on you. Something *not* good." His father put out a hand. "You took a souvenir, didn't you? Let's see it."

It finally dawned on Red what his father must be talking about. He reached into his back pocket and produced the wallet. Put it in his father's calloused hand.

The man turned it over, opened it, ran a fingertip along a stitched seam. He raised his eyebrows and frowned, whether in appreciation or disapproval, Red couldn't tell.

At last Don McCraith said, "These scales are the size of guitar picks. How big was this thing?"

"I didn't measure him, but I'm guessing 100 feet or so."

His father passed the wallet back. "Be careful with that, son." He shook his head and gave just the merest hint of a smile. "I ain't gonna tell you to be shed of it. But if I can sense it, there's others who can too. Some from this side, some from other places. Be mighty careful."

Red looked up at his father, still dazed and momentarily speechless.

His mother spoke up, "Your daddy was part of the Task Force when we met. I didn't like it, didn't even want to believe it. But I loved him, so…" She shrugged and went back to eating her breakfast.

His father picked up from there. "Your grandpa was a member, later on I was recruited, and looks like now it's your turn."

"Why didn't anyone tell me?"

Don McCraith laughed. "Would you have believed us?"

"When I was little, maybe."

"Yeah, and then you would've thought we were crazy. Just like I thought your grandpa was crazy and that photo a fake. Until, of course, I wound up in 'Nam and had my own run in with the Fae."

Red put his wallet away, then studied the photo. He looked up at his dad. "So tell me about it now. You never talk about what you saw over there. Maybe some of it'll help me."

"No!" said Don McCraith, firmly. "Ain't nothing I care to reminisce about. And don't exactly see how any of it would benefit you. Just keep your eyes open and take care of the men beside you, that's all any of you can do."

Red put the photo in his shirt pocket, alongside the medal. "Sorry, Daddy. Didn't mean to upset you. I just wanted—"

His father put up a hand, but gently, in a gesture of peace. "It's okay. Sometimes I just get...touchy." He looked at his son. "Or, as you called it, *defensive*." Then his voice caught a tremble. "Hell, maybe we're both just haunted by the past." He cleared his throat and whispered, "Inter Caelum et Infernum." As he went to spread jam on a biscuit, Don McCraith had tears welling in his eyes, but a smile creased his face. "Welcome home, son. I'm proud of you, and I love you."

Then his mother added, "Now try not to get killed by some sorcerer or demon and kindly get to eating your breakfast."

Chapter 16

December 18, 1990
Kerrsville, Georgia
0900 hours

Even though his visit was prompted by loss, it was a sweet time of reconnection. Still, Red was eager to get back to Djibouti. He'd already started bonding with the other JTF members and, given his varied background, had earned acceptance quickly. Which probably had more to do with his willingness to scrape barnacles, clean bright work, and keep the hull sanded and painted.

He was mentally preparing himself for the drive to Atlanta and the series of connecting flights that would put him back at Lemonnier, when the old rotary phone rang. His mother answered, then looked over.

"He's right here, sweetie." She handed him the phone and whispered, "Sounds cute. Whoever she is." She gave a "We'll talk later" look and walked away before he could respond.

Red put the receiver to his ear, wondering if this was some old girlfriend who heard he was in town. "Hello?"

"Petty Officer McCraith, this is…"

"Ensign Straub."

"First names are fine, Red. Glad you recognized my voice."

Maybe it was the few days at home, the familiarity of those who really knew him, but for whatever reason he found himself saying, "Tom. That's my actual name. You can call me Tom." He suddenly felt awkward, like he was being weird.

"Okay, Tom. I know you're with family, so I won't take long." If she'd picked up on any weirdness, it didn't reflect in her voice. "First, I'm really sorry about your grandfather. From what I've heard, he was an incredible person."

"More incredible by the day." Red put his fingers to his chest, pressing against the Purple Heart and photo inside his pocket.

"Second, during your layover in Virginia, I want to see you if possible."

"About the creature from the red lagoon, right?"

"The thing with a thousand nicknames, yeah." There was a hint of mirth in her tone. Then she got serious. "We're calling him Gurax. He claims to be an offspring of Dagon."

"Like our Operation. Makes sense."

"For more reasons than that. Which is part of what I need to tell you."

He paused, momentarily confused. "I thought you could just send intel via satellite."

Her voice took on a pensive tone, "We could encrypt it and ferry it over the airwaves. But that's my team over there, remember? My family. Even you, though we really didn't get to know one another at all."

"Sorry. I get what you're saying, and of course it makes sense. I'm stateside so you might as well reach out. I actually appreciate it. Just didn't expect it, is all."

"You have a two-hour layover. I'll find you and give you everything I've learned. Will that work?"

"Sounds good."

"See you soon, Tom. Oh, and don't be shocked when you notice something different about me."

"What would I—"

"I'm just trying to give you a heads up. Fair warning." She sounded exasperated. "Never mind. Just try not to make a big deal."

"Sure thing. Hey look, if you need my help or—"

"It's nothing like that. I'm just." She sighed. "Damn, I've gone and made things all weird."

"It's fine," he tried to assure her. "We caught Gurax with a high-tech cattle prod. Weird is our specialty. Our currency. Team Spooky, right?"

She laughed. "Yeah. Task Force Spooky. See you soon."

"See you, Cassie."

After he hung up, his mom poked her head back in the room. "If you tell me that was nobody, I'll have your daddy tan your hide for lying to your mama."

"She's a naval officer I met in Djibouti. Part of the Task Force."

His mom's eyes went wide. "Jah-booty? That some kind of Reggae red house? Oh Lord, my boy is gone and found himself a woman of ill repute."

Laughter erupted from the doorway. "Lucinda, honey. I love you but you are one sheltered lady."

"Just because I haven't been in every port across the world and walked through the red-light district, blue-light district, casinos, bars, and guts of all those cities, doesn't mean I'm naive."

"It's a country, Mama. Djibouti. Where I'm stationed in Africa."

Her face dimmed. "Oh. And this Cassie girl is your boss?"

"Might as well be," he said. "She outranks me by a long shot and always will. She works in intelligence now and has information for me to take back to the Team. That's all."

His dad walked into the room. He put his arms around Lucinda from behind, set his chin on her shoulder to smile over at his son. "Your mama outclassed me from day one. Always will. Maybe it's something like that."

Red realized his dad was messing with him, even though his mom wasn't. To both of them he said, "She's a fellow soldier. And I'm not looking for more."

"Just don't wait too long to settle down," said his mom. "I want some grandkids to spoil." His dad just grinned and winked, his head still on her shoulder.

Chapter 17

December 18, 1990
Dulles International Airport, Virginia
1600 hours

Red traveled in uniform, to help facilitate things along the way. It seemed to garner a measure of friendly rapport during check-in at the airport. He flew from Atlanta to Virginia, grabbed his bags from the overhead and made his way to the food court near his next terminal, where he assumed he'd meet Cassie.

He was almost there when he noticed her, walking resolutely toward him and smiling wide.

He noticed too, the right sleeve of her uniform pinned up at the elbow. A bag was slung across that shoulder. He smiled back, intentionally kept his eyes on her face, even as he wondered what the hell had happened. Since they were both in uniform, he saluted.

As they drew close, Cassie returned his salute with her left hand and said, "Let's talk about this before it turns into some kind of elephant in the room."

"Exactly," Red agreed, making a show of staring at her collar. "Guess Belfry was right about that promotion after all. Congratulations, Lieutenant Junior Grade."

She motioned to a table by a burger place. "Nice try. Let's sit, and I'll tell you what happened." Cassie walked over, unslung the bag and sat it on the ground. She sat in the chair beside it.

Red took the chair opposite her. Once he'd been filled in, his expression went dark. "This is my fault. I stepped away from the plan and you paid the price." He cursed himself mentally. History was repeating itself.

Cassie reached into her bag and pulled out a folder. She placed it on the table between them. "Save it. I wasn't paying attention and the bastard got me. It's that simple."

"I left the net on the deck," he reminded her. "If we'd hauled that thing up in it, like we planned, you'd still have your arm."

"Drop it, Petty Officer." She glared at him. "I don't need your sympathy, and laying blame doesn't help either of us. This—" She stabbed her index down on the folder. "This is what we're going to discuss now, so pay attention and relay it to the others."

Red blinked. She was right, of course, but it didn't change the way he felt. Still, he pushed the issue aside and refocused. "Sorry. What have you learned?"

She opened the folder, took out the first sheet, and pushed it his way.

He pulled it in close and spun it around. It was a reproduction of an old map, a depiction of the world's oceans, filled with intricate drawings of fantastic creatures. He expected to find inscriptions of 'here be dragons', but that particular detail was absent.

"No doubt you've seen this before, or similar types," she said.

He nodded. "Old maritime cartography. Mythical monsters to explain things the sailors had no words for."

"That's a replica of the Carta Marina, made in the Renaissance era. In the sixteenth century, 1539 to be exact. An exiled Swedish priest named Olaus Magnus made this in Venice to explain North Sea creatures to a group of Italians." She pointed to a specific image. "According to Magnus, this red sea serpent was 200 feet long."

The drawing depicted a serpentine creature wrapping itself around an old sailing ship, a carrack by the look of its hull. The creature's mouth hung open, as if ready to devour the crew. "Reminds me of the Yacumama," he said. "Only bigger."

"Bigger is right," she said. "And imagine that map on a sheet about five and a half by four feet."

Red arched an eyebrow. "Was this Magnus fellow trying to aid exploration or end it?"

She laughed. "Haven't thought of it that way. Maybe the latter. Magnus did claim the appearance of the sea serpent meant something bad was about to happen. How did he put it?" She scrunched her nose in thought, then quoted, '...the Princes shall die, or be banished; or some Tumultuous Wars shall presently follow.'"

"Alrighty then." He passed the map back. "What else do you have?"

"We're talking with Gurax." She pulled out the next sheet.

"You're kidding me." He took the paper, which appeared to be a transcript.

"Read that," she said, "I'm going to grab one of those burgers." She stood. "You want something?"

"You bet." He leaned forward and pulled out his wallet.

"That's okay, I've got it," she said.

He fished out a twenty. "Not trying to pull any chauvinist crap, but Papa would turn in his grave if I let a lady get the tab."

She shook her head with a wry smile. "In deference to your recent loss, I'll let you play the dead grandpa card." She took the twenty and added, "*This* time. But next one's on me."

Then she spotted the wallet. "Still got the hide I see."

"Surprised you didn't sense it already," he said. "And I'll have mine all the way, Swiss cheese if they've got it, American if they don't."

She watched as he slipped the wallet away. "Oh, I sensed it. I've just spent so much time around Gurax that I've almost grown accustomed to the aura. And I'll make sure you get your change."

He waved a hand. "No need. Just leave a tip with the rest."

She nodded. "Read that transcript. I think we're gonna have a few things to iron out when I get back. One being that wallet." She turned and went to order.

Red watched her go, realizing the wallet trophy was about to cause more friction. Then he noticed the way her hips moved and caught himself. "Mama's done put thoughts in my head," he muttered as he looked at the transcript. He was curious as to its contents, but also curious about *other* things. He shook his head, and started reading:

Straub: You claim you are Gurax, spawn of the Babylonian god Dagon? And you serve Saxüru?

Gurax: Yes.

Straub: Saxüru is an enemy. He fights humans. Seeks to kill humans.

Gurax: Saxüru is not fighting humans now. First Saxüru must fight the enemy of my kind. He wishes to work with humans to fight this enemy. Human warriors and warriors of Saxüru will fight this enemy together.

Straub: Humans will not serve Saxüru. The kingdom of Babylon is gone. Human weapons will destroy Saxüru, and any enemy that dares to attack us.

Gurax: Humans are not the most powerful. The Ancient ones awaken. They will kill all—Saxüru, humans, all.

Straub: What are the names of these ancients?

Gurax: Many. Dendan. Tennyn.

Straub: We humans do not trust Saxüru.

Gurax: Saxüru does not trust humans.

Straub: And still, you want human warriors to fight alongside the warriors of Saxüru, to kill this common enemy.

Gurax: Yes. First, we must kill the Ancients.

Straub: And once these Ancients are dead, then there will be peace between humans and Saxüru?

Gurax: No. After Ancients are dead, Saxüru will take his rightful place. Saxüru will rule the humans.

Straub: And if we refuse to submit to his rule?

Gurax: Then Saxüru will kill humans until he is given the honor and worship he is due.

Cassie returned with the food. "Now, about that wallet," she said as she set the tray down.

"You want me to hand it over."

She frowned. "I'm not the only one who sensed it. Back at sea, Gurax and that merman we killed both did."

Red unwrapped his burger and started in. "Um. Not possible, didn't exactly have it in my wetsuit."

"Nevertheless, it wasn't chum that lured them in, even if it was spiked with your blood. Though you weren't carrying it on you, that Yacumama hide left traces of the supernatural on you."

"Is that somewhere in this transcript?"

"About three pages down." She started in on her own burger.

"Okay, but about this first page. I get the gist of it, the creature wants to ally itself with us to fight a common enemy, but then it'll turn on us. He also mentions Dendan and Tennyn. What are those?"

She finished her bite then answered, "A giant fish and a giant sea serpent."

"Like the ones on the map."

"Exactly. The word Tennyn is Arabic, but its variant is found in the Jewish scriptures which were later translated into Latin and finally English to comprise part of the Christian Bible. The word *Dagon* is preserved in the English translation, the Hebrew *Tanniyn* isn't. But it's still there."

"So how is Tanniyn translated?" Red took another bite.

"Dragon, serpent, whale, and sea monster in the King James Old Testament."

"Take your pick, huh?"

Cassie nodded. "Now let's go over the rest. There are some reproductions of ancient carvings that tie into what you'll be facing, more transcripts, and—most importantly—where all this seems to be heading. Keep in mind, some of these sources give conflicting info. Not all folklore is accurate or complete."

Red shrugged. "Just like our everyday, garden-variety Intel."

She smiled. "Something like that." She started back on her food.

He found himself smiling back, then looking away before it turned into a stare. Her blue eyes were as striking as ever. She was talking about the intel again. And though Red tried really hard to pay attention to the words, her flawless skin and perfect lips were so *damn* distracting.

They finished just as Red's plane began boarding. "It was good to see you again," he said.

She put out her left hand. "Same." As he shook it, she added, "And I'll have to ask you to hand over that wallet. It may put you at risk."

"Seriously? I can't keep a snakeskin wallet that I made myself, from a monster I killed myself?"

She sighed. "Please don't make me order you."

"Lieutenant... Cassie, c'mon. I grew up in podunk Georgia. I've killed and eaten wild game since I was nine or ten. I've got a knife back home with a handle made of deer antler. When I was twelve, I killed my first gator. Wasn't legal, of course, but we did eat the tail, and I've still got a belt made of its hide. Daddy's got a nice pair of boots..."

"I have orders to find out exactly what it was that drew Gurax to you. It would help if I could present the item outright."

He tried a different tactic. "But it's where I keep my folding money."

"I'm getting the tab next time, remember?"

He was at a loss. "Right."

She smiled. "Tell you what, hand over the wallet and maybe there will actually be a next time."

He scratched his head. "Is that a promise or a threat? Or a date?"

"Maybe all three." She put her hand out again.

Red carefully pulled everything from his wallet and shifted it all to a zippered pouch in his pack. Finally, he handed the snakeskin over.

She took it, then motioned to the folder and its contents. "Take those with you. Use them to brief the rest of the team."

"Got it." He shuffled all the papers back into the folder, then opened his pack and slipped it in.

The loudspeaker announced final boarding.

Cassie slipped the wallet under what was left of her her right arm and stood to go. "I'll be in touch. You take care and tell the guys I've got their backs at HQ."

Red stood. "Sure thing." He slung his pack to his shoulder and saluted.

Reflexively Cassie moved her right arm, dropping the wallet. "Well shit," she said, staring numbly at the floor.

Red knelt to pick it up. "My fault," he said. "Wasn't thinking." He slipped it into the bag still by her chair, then picked that up and handed it to her.

"No," she said, taking the bag. "Things have changed. Still figuring it all out. Got to remember to salute left-handed."

"Pick your nose left-handed," Red offered, in an attempt at levity.

"Wipe left-handed," she countered.

He held up his palms. "Too much info. You win." He smiled as he tried to find a way to say goodbye. "I hate this happened to you. But I've also seen what you're made of. You're gonna do fine, *Lieutenant JG*."

"Thanks, Tom. Catch you next time."

"See you, Cassie."

Chapter 18

December 19, 1990
Camp Lemonnier
1700 hours

As soon as he was back at Lemonnier, Red met with everyone in the briefing room. Though official 'duty hours' were ending, he wanted to fill them in right away. The trip had taken roughly 17 hours plus a 7-hour difference in time zones. He'd napped during the first bit of the flight and was eager to match his sleep cycle with the others. He set the 8x10 sheets depicting various engraved images out across the table, and got to work explaining their significance, along with Gurax's transcript.

Once he finished, Hank said, "Let me get this straight. Saxüru, or whatever he wants to call himself, expects us to find him, then help him out, knowing the whole time he's gonna turn on us the moment this common enemy is destroyed? And we're gonna do it?"

Red shrugged. "Sounds crazy, but that's the impression I got."

"Sounds like standard operating procedure to me," offered Waymore.

Hank snorted. "You've got me there." He looked to Red. "You said '*impression*'. So you weren't given any specific orders?"

Red caught the drift, finally realizing the subtlety of Cassie's approach. "Lieutenant Junior Grade Straub wasn't explicit with any orders. Just seemed to be sharing info. Though I got the sense orders would be forthcoming."

Hank's eyes narrowed as he rubbed his chin thoughtfully. "She's looking out for us, is what she's doing."

"Her *and* Morrison," offered Belfry.

"About Morrison..." Red raised a brow. "What's his connection to this little outpost?"

"Here's the quick and dirty," said Hank. "He saved two of our guys from a collision at sea. A water dragon in the middle of the Triangle of all places."

"That thing would've killed half the ship," said Belfry.

"Or all of it," said Doc.

"Way I hear it, he took a fall for doing the right thing," Waymore continued, "So an arrogant jerk could save face and the Task Force could keep things under wraps."

"Most of us only met him after he recruited us," said Shiv. "When nobody else would believe us or wanted to send us packing with a Section 8, Morrison showed up."

"He offered us the opportunity to either be reassigned, with no mention of what we'd experienced," said Hank. "Or—"

"A chance to fight the demons of Hell itself," Slim finished for his captain.

Hank grinned. "A bit dramatic, but close enough. Now then," he said, "Let's get clear on our next move."

Red spoke up again, "Cassie said Saxüru speaks some ancient Babylonian tongue, so we might need an interpreter."

Waymore started laughing. "Don't need a damn interpreter."

"All we need is a mug shot," said Belfry.

Red selected a sheet from the table. "Here's the closest thing to a mug shot she could give me."

Though they'd all seen it already, Hank took the page for a closer look. He frowned at the image, a creature with the upper body of a goat and a fish-like tail. The face was a menacing snarl.

"Great. We're supposed to make a deal with some water demon." Hank passed the sheet along.

Johnson took it. As he sent it down the line, he said, "Looks like the devil himself, if you ask me."

Waymore gave it a cursory glance. "Like I said, business as usual."

Belfry was uncharacteristically serious. "So, we gonna chum the waters again?"

Hank said, "We drop anchor where we bagged sushi and crab cakes, then send him a personal invite." He looked to Waymore. "You outfit that probe yet?"

"We'll get his attention."

Red spoke up, "I feel like I'm missing something. What exactly are we saying here?"

"We're being proactive," said Hank. "Ain't gonna be no deals with any devils, human or otherwise. Every time we go that route one of ours takes the fall or pays the ultimate price. So, what we're gonna do is tap on Satan's shoulder then unload on his ass."

Red understood.

"Cut off the head." Shiv spoke up, hand propped on the 45 at her hip. "Got a problem with that?"

Red smiled. "I'm mister *'ask forgiveness not permission'*, remember?"

Hank put a hand on Red's shoulder. "We're given a lot of leeway out here, to make these waters safe as we can. Run interference so the conventional side can do its job unhindered. That said, if we get orders counter to our current plan, we act accordingly and obey those orders." He looked around at the team, "So, let's get moving and kill this bastard before some bureaucrat comes up with a 'better' idea."

It wasn't exactly a runaround on the chain of command. Hank simply made a proactive assessment and reached out to the fleet, offering help. This met with quick acceptance from a fleet officer who was 'read in' on JTF13 and recognized the value of such an offer.

The move, though not entirely selfless, wasn't so far outside protocol to arouse suspicion. It might even be enough to deflect concerns when they delivered or reported a *dead* Saxüru. They just needed to move fast, before they got orders to cooperate with the damn thing or bring it in alive.

They were underway inside twenty-four hours of Red's return. "I've briefed the others," Hank told him as they left port. "And we're all in agreement: you brought us this Intel. You deserve to take point."

Red gazed out the window to the sea. "Our plan's a good one. And Shiv's backup plan is solid."

"When we engage, you're taking the first shot. And if that bastard doesn't go down, we're gonna unload, so get out of the way. We're not gonna play it safe. Nor are we gonna wing it and make last minute adjustments unless we need to."

Red nodded. "Roger that."

They entered the Red Sea through the Gate of Tears. During his previous few transits, Red had a fairly easy go, in terms of environmental conditions. This time he quickly discovered what everyone else had told him; expect the wind and seas to be against them regardless of the previous day or even the time of year. They shot through the strait in the middle of a fierce squall.

Red was on the quarterdeck, learning the finer points of Hydrofoil navigation from Shiv. Shiv was on the headphones scanning the charts and radar. "Small contact," she called to Johnson, who was manning the wheel. "Straight ahead."

Red strained to see in the darkness. Visibility was poor, with the wind blowing up a heavy brown spume.

"How close?" Johnson asked.

"A little over a hundred yards."

Shiv was deceptively calm at her nav station. Red took the initiative and flipped the switch on a forward searchlight. A beam lit up the blackness.

The contact was a fisherman, standing up in a small fishing vessel. He was hauling a net, his boat completely unlit. Probably doing some illegal fishing under cover of night.

Hank, acting officer of the deck, spoke up, "Steer clear of that net. Hard to starboard."

"Hard to starboard, aye," said Johnson, steering suddenly to the east.

The fishing boat passed close along the port side when Shiv said, "More contacts, closing fast, starboard bow."

Using binocs, Hank gauged the cluster of boats entering the searchlight. "Helm, get them further starboard."

This time there were four small, unlit vessels. "Steering to port," Johnson answered, turning the wheel. The *Scorpius* was in the narrowest part of the channel. The current and waves worked against them.

Shiv looked up from her scope. "That should be it for a while. Good job, Johnson." The boats passed to starboard. She checked position on the chart and quickly got her face back to the scope.

The rest of the night was uneventful. Shift change was around 0600 hours. They completed the first arc of their journey and prepared to drop anchor at noon.

Though sailors of old always hugged the eastern shore to avoid the worst of the wind and currents, the plotted course of the *Scorpius* was a hop-scotched PIM up the coast along the Sea's western side. Since a direct approach would definitely raise eyebrows, their series of stops was an intentional effort to avoid a straight shot to their destination. They needed to hurry without looking like they were.

Chapter 19

December 21, 1990
The Red Sea
1600 hours

As the days passed, the *Scorpius* repeated the process, anchoring in the ancient, yet beautiful bays—marsas, as the Arabs called them. Had they had more time, they would have gone diving. According to Waymore, the reefs in the area were among the best in the world.

The intent was to keep close to shore, to run interference for the fleet if needed. Tensions were high in the region: Hussein had yet to back out of Kuwait, and the buildup of U.S. vessels suggested America was getting ready to push the Iraqis out.

The conventional ships were strategically situated; anchored or staying in assigned sectors for missile strikes, should the time come. The *Scorpius* would flank the US warships, keeping to the western edge of the Sea on their trek northward to the point where they planned to deploy the probe.

They'd engage Saxüru there, complete their mission, then steam on until they neared the Suez Canal. At that point, the *Scorpius* would turn around for a final sweep back toward Djibouti, keeping to the eastern side of the Sea on their return leg.

Their immediate goal, of course, was a spot near the center of the Sea, Sudan to the west and Mecca due east.

The first half of their trek took them along the coast of Eritrea. Red was on the weather deck, staring toward the shore when Hank joined him at the rail. Off duty, the marine was attired in casual work denims and a black t-shirt. He pointed at the port city in the distance. "That's Massawa."

Red nodded. "Eritrea. Aren't they at war with Ethiopia?"

"Since '61. Back in February their People's Liberation Front recaptured Massawa. Then the leader of Ethiopia, Meningitis Hail Marijane, or something like that, hit it with napalm and cluster bombs." Hank swept his hand along the coast. "It's like that on both sides of this godforsaken stretch of water. Sudan has Omar al-Bashir. Came to power last year. Was a brigadier in their Army and led a military coup. Rumor has it he's your basic genocidal dictator."

Red shrugged. "At least there's Egypt."

Hank grinned. "Yeah, let's not forget Egypt. Nine political parties, with a never-ending presidential *state of emergency*."

"But hey, at least the Saudi's are stable." Red barely got the words out before a snort of laughter escaped his lips.

Hank chuckled as he followed up with, "Yemen… no place like Yemen."

Red composed himself, still smiling. "Remind me again… just what in the *hell* are we doing over here?"

Hank slapped him on the back. "Saving the world, son. Demon killing devils that's what we are." He grew serious and said, "You know they call *us* devils, right?"

"Sure. Devil dogs. It's practically a Marine Corps mascot."

"No, not that. The Arabs that know about *us*." He touched the JTF-13 patch, sewn onto the t-shirt, over his left pec. "They call the Task Force *Thlatht Eshr Shayatin*, the Thirteen Devils."

Red raised an eyebrow. "Nice. And when do I get one of those t-shirts?"

With a tilt of his head and a half-smirk, Hank said, "Ain't gonna look as cool on you, but I'll see what we can do." He started back inside. "Now let's get moving. Got a demi-god to kill, or whatever that thing is."

As soon as they were underway again, Red was reminded he couldn't let his guard down in the Red Sea. Instead of demi-gods or mermen, this time he faced his first sandstorm. He was still on the weather decks when it seemed to rage up out of nowhere.

"Seriously?" he said, pulling the bridge door closed. "A sandstorm on the water?"

"More frequent than you'd expect," said Shiv.

"Didn't expect it at all," he retorted.

"Exactly," said Belfry.

Hank got on the intercom, "Weather decks are secured. All hands, take shelter and secure exterior doors and hatches."

With a quickly deteriorating weather window, the *Scorpius* pulled into a bay that was completely surrounded by desert and dropped anchor again. The wind rose to 35 knots, turning the air orange with blown sand.

Soon the deck was covered with it. Through the bridge windows, Red noticed sand clinging to the grease in their winches and chocks.

Hank cursed the sharp, gritty sand as the wind blew in tight, unrelenting circles. "Makes me sick just to think about it. One minute of this is like a month of usual wear and tear. Nothing like having your vessel sandblasted while you wait out the storm."

When it finally abated, they hosed everything off as well as they could and started moving again. One more stop before they reached their destination, but they needed to get there soon.

Red was on the aft end of the *Scorpius* staring at a Marsa shore littered with the corpses of goats, dogs, donkeys, and a host of creatures desiccated beyond recognition.

Shiv came up beside him. "Got a bad feeling about this, Red. Like something doesn't want us to complete this mission."

"So, this is unusual?"

She sighed. "Not really. The animals wander across the desert, slowly dying of thirst. They probably see water mirages all the time. Then they happen upon the bays, can't believe their eyes, and stumble down to the salt water to drink. It's probably delicious, for a moment or two. But then they start cramping, topple over, and writhe in pain until they die."

"Well that's encouraging." Red frowned at the scene. "I'm ready to get there. Get this over."

"You're good, Red," Shiv conceded, "but you've been damn lucky too. And luck runs out. So, don't get complacent, okay?"

"I know." He gripped the heavy cable that served as a top rail, threaded through the posts along either side of the ship. "So, do me a favor and watch my back, help keep me in line."

"Got a better idea," she said, "I'll help you *hold* the line." With that she turned to go. "Gonna catch some shuteye. Best you do the same."

"Wilco," he said, as she rounded the corner. Red turned back to the shoreline.

And was shocked to see a man robed in desert attire, standing in the midst of the fallen animals. The man was tall, dark-skinned, and sported a flowing beard. In one hand he held a long staff of pale, gnarled wood.

Like a mirage, the man shimmered in the heat rising from the desert sands. Without a sound, he raised his staff, swatches of cloth billowing as he gestured.

Even across the distance, Red could sense the man's piercing yellow gaze, unblinking, as they stared at each other. The man held the staff aloft, his lips began to move as if muttering an incantation or prayer. Red half-expected the waters to begin parting from one shore to the other.

"What the hell?" he whispered.

"You okay, bud?"

Red snapped around to face the voice.

Hank stood at the corner where Shiv had departed. "Everything all right?"

Red turned back to the strange, dark-skinned wizard.

And saw nothing but a corpse littered beach again.

He strained for a sign of the wanderer, but there was nothing. Not even a dark smudge of the man walking away, receding into the distance. No sign he was ever there.

"Uh...Yeah," Red finally said. "I'm fine. Everything's...just fine."

"Tomorrow's the big day," said Hank, "And we're on in seven hours, so go get some rest. That's an order."

Absently, Red nodded. "Yes sir." He turned from the rail and made his way to his hammock.

John S. Worth

Chapter 20

December 22, 1990
The Red Sea
1330 hours

Waymore chunked the probe over the side. "Fire in the hole!" It splashed and took off, its propulsion activated by water hitting a sensor in an access port.

Hank leaned back, pushing mirrored shades into place. "Thing's faster than I thought."

"Everybody stand by." Red shouldered his rifle. "If those coordinates are accurate, we're either gonna float a body to the surface or have one very pissed demon-fish-goat-demigod." He had his finger outside the trigger guard, but the safety was off and the selector set to full auto.

The probe was a hodgepodge of state-of-the-art tech and underwater demolition. Using coordinates provided by Red as relayed by Cassie, divulged by an overconfident Gurax, the weapon would drop within fifteen meters of Saxüru's 'abode', or so they hoped. Upon reaching that point, the blast should be more than enough to shatter his bones.

Unless, of course, Gurax's lack of concern was warranted.

John S. Worth

Down in the brine, deep in the trenches, Saxüru sat upon the jagged ridge. With his own cloven paws, he'd cracked and hewn the rock into a makeshift throne. He expected to hear from Gurax soon.

Then he felt the disturbance. A vibration in the waters, not unlike the mechanical vessels of modern humans. But this was on a much smaller scale. He smiled. Finally, the humans were coming to him.

A churning sound and he turned just in time to see it. Oblong as an egg of the great sea serpent and gray as the murky depths, it sped his way. Saxüru bent his head, as if preparing to ram it with his horns, and waited.

The egg-thing whirred close enough for Saxüru to touch it. He reached out, curiosity getting the better of him. In that moment, it came violently apart, sending metal fragments and shockwaves in all directions.

The blast sent Saxüru reeling, as the water turned black. Struggling to hold onto consciousness, he pawed at the ridge as he tumbled past, desperately seeking purchase. He realized the dark cloud roiling through the brine was his own blood.

Then his back slammed hard against the seafloor, whiplashing his head into the rocky bottom. Saxüru fought back nausea, determined to remain conscious. For a moment he lay there, on the edge of darkness, waiting for his strength to return and his head to clear. He moved a feeble arm from his chest and pushed against the ridge. Finally, he propped himself into a sitting position. He began to undulate his tail fin, and slowly arose, holding himself upright.

A quick scan suggested no bones were broken. He moved his limbs and flicked his tail to confirm the fact. But a gash marked his forearm where he'd foolishly reached out for the human weapon, for he realized now — too late — what the object had been.

Another moment and his heart lurched, as he noticed something down on the seabed, slowly rocking with the churning water. A large, curled horn tumbled away with the undercurrent. He reached up to run a cloven paw across his skull.

His anger erupted in a scream of fury, which called out through the depths for every lurking creature to hear. His right horn had sheared off near its base. Saxüru, God of the Red Sea, was forever disfigured.

He took in great gulps of water, breathing hard, gathering oxygen into his bloodstream. He stretched out, racing toward the horn. Reaching down, he grabbed it, as he swam past, wielding the broken fragment of himself like a dagger.

Saxüru turned his face toward the surface. Gripping the horn, he ignored the blood still sluicing from his torn flesh. He'd carried such wounds before. His arm would heal. The horn, however, would not. Calling out for reinforcements, he raced up from the depths, determined to make the humans pay.

Shiv finished prepping her M60. "Feel that?" she asked.

And suddenly Red did. A furtive glance confirmed they all felt it, as rounds were chambered, and weapons readied. Anyone who'd encountered the supernatural could sense the air crackling with an emanation of pure evil.

"Even my scrotum hair's on edge," Belfry muttered.

No one laughed. They were too focused on the oppressive aura headed their way.

Water shot into the air not fifty yards from the *Scorpius*. A massive beast rose with the eruption, as if riding atop a huge column of water.

The moment he saw it, Red agreed whole-heartedly with Johnson's assessment. This was Satan in the flesh. He put an M249 SAW to his shoulder, sighted the creature, and opened fire.

Before the onslaught of lead could rip through the creature's hide, Saxüru was gone. The thing moved with unnatural speed. In a blur, it struck out from the spray to skitter across the surface in a jagged line.

Red adjusted, tried to lead his target, laying down a steady stream till his belt emptied.

"Deuces, yer up!" Hank shouted.

Red fell back, dropping behind Johnson and Waymore, who stepped up to the fifty cals temporarily swivel-mounted on their stanchions on either side of the bridge. Shiv stood on the aft deck, firing a Pig from her shoulder to lay down cover and keep anything from getting too close.

Johnson and Waymore opened fire as the sea erupted again. Saltwater sprayed as winding geysers burst from the surface like a dozen incipient hurricanes. Both men lost sight of their target and ceased fire as the *Scorpius* pitched on a sudden swell.

Hank shouted above the din as waves crashed over the side, "Everyone in! Let's spit some shells and get on the foils."

Not two seconds later the crew was on the bridge, reassessing.

Red gave an exasperated huff. "Son of a bitch is fast!"

"And what the hell are those waterspouts?" asked Waymore.

"Merfolk. Counted four of them," Shiv answered. "Plus the biggest croc I've ever seen and a damned puffer fish wide as a Buick."

Hank stayed focused on the objective. He keyed the mic that would relay to his fire controlman. "Belfry, get a lock and kill that bastard."

The forward mount swung into play, even as the foils were deployed.

The weapon pounded out shells in a swinging arc, mowing down two mermen and deflating the puffer fish even as it shredded the thing's dorsal fin.

The *Scorpius* surged forward, seeming to rise above the sea. At the helm, Slim poured on the speed until they broke free of the area. Spray coated the deck as the hydrofoils kicked up water on both sides of the ship's wake.

Behind them, Saxüru mounted the monstrous crocodile, wedging himself into the ridge plates of the monster's back.

"Get ready to harpoon that bastard," Hank said through gritted teeth.

Even as fast as the *Scorpius* was, it was apparent the great reptile would soon match speed and catch up. The monster was bigger than any gator Red had ever seen. He estimated its length at fifty feet, with eyes that glowed with an otherworldly eeriness. Its mouth parted slightly, exposing rows of weathered, yellow teeth. Like ragged stalactites lining the roof of a cave.

"Can't let that thing get close." Red muttered aloud.

"Don't intend to," said Hank. "Don't wanna pit our hull against those jaws."

"And don't underestimate the tail. Thing could bust us wide open."

Dunc spared a sideways glance. "Sounds like you've been up close and personal."

"A few times."

Johnson raised his eyebrows. "Would've figured you for a sheep man, but hey. Each to his own."

Hank suppressed a grin. "Enough of that." He keyed the squawk box connecting him to the Fire Control station. "Belfry, anytime you're ready."

"Harpoon locked on target," came Belfry's reply.

"Fire!"

Belfry worked his controls. "Happy Hanukkah, you cross-bred abomination." A million dollars worth of firepower flashed from the aft deck, as a harpoon missile streamed into the air, quickly followed by another.

Chapter 21

December 22, 1990
The Red Sea
1340 hours

Saxüru watched as two of his servants were struck down by streaming volleys of metal. The fish was surely dead. He urged the reptile forward, chattering at it to close the gap, to get him within reach. He used his own severed horn as a spike. Gripped in one fist and lodged between two ridges, it helped him keep his perch.

Then he saw the blast and caught a fleeting glimpse of another weapon. Large and fast. Another flash.

He wrenched his horn free and dove, plunging into the water even as his mount was ripped apart. The shockwave caught up before he could escape, slamming into him like an iron fist. For the second time that day, he found himself tumbling uncontrollably in the very element he ruled.

Though he fought for control, another blast rocked the sea again. Its vibrations rattled his spine. This time the darkness would not be denied. Saxüru's grip loosened, the curved spike fell away, and, for the first time in eons, the Babylonian god was defeated. The brine pulled him down, as all else faded to black.

The *Scorpius* sped above the waves at an unbelievable 45 knots. Red was awestruck. To read the spec sheet was one thing, but the experience was something altogether more.

"It's like we're flying!" he exclaimed, in spite of himself and the ordeal they'd just survived.

Hank smiled wide, acknowledging the moment. "Nothing like the first time."

Johnson slapped Red on the back. "Tonight, we celebrate."

Hank reined them in; "Before we bust out the champagne, how bout we steer back and see if we can find what's left of Billy Goat Gruff?"

"Roger that," said Slim, taking it as an order. The ship turned in a wide arc, throwing up a sheet of water. Then the hydrofoil slowed as it approached the scene of engagement. The *Scorpius* dropped back down, hull in the sea, as the foils folded away. They crept ahead at 10 knots, still wary, even though the Harpoon missile was enough to take out a full-sized warship.

"Everyone, scour the surface," said Hank, opening the door to the weather deck. "Shiv, you watch that scope."

"Aye sir," she said, settling in above it.

Out on the weather deck, the crew split into four groups of two: forward, aft, port, and starboard.

Once they were sure there was no immediate threat, they began a search pattern, looking for a carcass or whatever remains they could find. Though no one believed Saxüru had survived a harpoon missile, they all wanted proof the thing was dead.

An hour passed with no such confirmation. Dunc finally managed to hook the fin of the puffer fish. The rest had broken off, drifted away or sank.

"Careful not to touch anything bare handed," said Hank. They all knew what happened to Cassie. "Matter of fact, best just leave it alone."

"Shouldn't we at least take samples?" Red asked.

Waymore shook his head. "Not sure what the brass is gonna think of our little run-in. And do we really want to hand over stuff that might give the Intel side any crazy ideas?"

"What's our mission again?" Red prodded.

"What are you raving about?" asked Waymore. "We kill devils and fight back evil."

Red reminded them of his wallet. And what Cassie had told about that particular souvenir. "No telling what she's found out by now. And what she can probably do with anything we send her way."

"The Secondary Mission *is* investigative," Hank conceded. "To understand the unknown, to reach into the dark and pull back the truth." He sighed. "Even so, I'm not so sure we didn't just dodge a bullet." He nodded to Red. "It's your idea, and you seem to be versed in the skinning department, so we're gonna haul in a few fragments and let you do the honors."

"Yes sir." Red turned to Dunc, pulling on a pair of gloves and fetching his knife from its sheath. "Haul that fin over here."

"Got a piece of that croc on this side," said Johnson.

"Grab a net and dip it up," said Hank.

The door to the quarterdeck opened and Slim stuck out his head. "Shiv's got radio contact with the fleet. Some destroyer captain saw our missile and has a few questions."

Hank sighed. "I'll handle it." He looked to the men still on the deck. "Get a piece of the fish and skin some hide off that croc. Then put it all on ice, wash up, and meet in twenty to debrief."

"Yes sir," said Belfry, holding a speared dorsal fin steady while Red grabbed it with a gloved hand. "Christmas presents for the Intel brass."

A report was filed with headquarters. The *Scorpius's* crew completed their trek around the Red Sea, hoping like hell they'd killed Saxüru, since their report clearly stated the creature could not have survived the blast. It was a safe assertion, especially when the croc itself was blown apart.

Photos were included, of course, along with the tissue samples from the puffer fish and croc. Ultimately, no follow-up orders were given to actively seek out any specific supernatural creatures. They were to provide support to the Fleet and, in Hank's words, "Continue to hold the line." Which they did.

The next few months were uneventful. Then, mid-January of '91, the hell they'd all been expecting broke loose.

Chapter 22

January 5, 1991
The Red Sea, deep in the trenches

Saxüru could not tell if it was loyalty or fear that had motivated the merfolk to save him. It pleased him to think perhaps a mixture of both drove their actions.

After he was knocked unconscious, the two remaining mermen managed to find him, lying still on the seabed, his left arm broken and everything else bruised or torn. One of them also managed to retrieve his broken horn, no doubt hoping to curry favor.

He awoke in an undersea cavern. Many tides had passed. Though they could not tell him exactly how many, there had been enough that his broken arm, lashed with thick seaweed against a splint fashioned from the wreckage of a sailing vessel, had almost mended.

They brought him shark flesh, crabs, and squid to eat. Saxüru was weak and his body so long without food the offerings roused nausea instead of hunger. Still, he knew he must regain his strength.

Then he would seek out the vessel that nearly killed him. It was so fast and its weapons so powerful. He had never seen anything like it. He would find where it ported. That was the only way. Catch the humans unaware and make them pay. Slowly, he forced himself to eat.

His servants, however, seemed overly concerned with another matter. One Saxüru had all but forgotten.

"The fissure," said one. "It widens. The great fish pounds against it and may soon break through."

The other added, "Neither Gurax nor Xin has returned. They are surely dead. We must gather our kindred and prepare for war against the great fish."

The first spoke again, "Dendan is unlike any of the beasts you command. He serves no one and will feed upon us all."

The last statement roused Saxüru's anger. Though weakened, he lashed out with his good arm and grabbed his servant by the throat. "I do not fear Dendan. Just as I do not fear the humans. I will kill the great fish before he can even escape his prison. But first I will feast on the humans." He glared at the man-fish as it fought helplessly for breath, unable to draw water through the gills clamped tight beneath Saxüru's cloven hoof.

The demi-god chattered ominously, "Perhaps I should start by feasting on you."

He tightened his grip, brought the underling close and opened his mouth. Saxüru grinned, exposing wide teeth, the pointed ends razor sharp. He snapped once in the creature's face, causing it to flinch. Finally, he flung it aside, releasing his hold.

"Speak again to me of Dendan, and I will kill you both."

Chapter 23

January 17, 1991
The Red Sea
early morning hours

Nine ships in the Mediterranean Sea, Arabian Gulf, and Red Sea fire the first Tomahawk missiles during Operation Desert Storm, marking the first combat launch of the weapon. Guided-missile cruiser *San Jacinto* fires the first from the Red Sea, while guided-missile cruiser *Bunker Hill* fires the first from the Arabian Gulf. Fast attack submarines USS *Louisville* and USS *Pittsburgh* fire the first submarine-launched Tomahawks. By the end of day three, United States ships and submarines will have launched 216 missiles against 17 Iraqi targets.

The call to battle stations was devoid of the blaring 1MC announcements and hurried scuttle of larger ships. For the *Scorpius*, it was a 'General Quarters' message repeated twice over the intercom, simply stated and with no sirens or flashing lights.

The off-duty crew simply responded by joining their counterparts at whatever station they were assigned. The crew of twelve took less than one minute to muster.

Once everyone was at their post, Hank made his rounds, informing everyone of the reason for their course change. "We just tomahawked the hell out of Baghdad. We're taking station with the southernmost ships."

Like the ships around it, the destroyer unleashed hell on a distant enemy. A Tomahawk lit up its deck and the sky as it raced through the air at over five hundred miles-per-hour. Weighing one and a half tons, each missile could strike within a meter of a target a thousand miles away. The opening salvos, in a war that started six months earlier, delivered a message loud and clear:

We're done talking. Get out of Kuwait.

Though the waters were calm during the initial launch, as the Vertical Launching System (VLS) began hot ejection of the third missile, a massive wave came out of nowhere.

The captain didn't have time to cease fire on the Tomahawk. The water caught it just as it cleared the VLS, spun it around and shoved it against the starboard rail.

The sea churned, pitching the ship suddenly.

As the captain ordered the ceasefire, another huge wave lifted the ship. The destroyer crested that wave then dropped headlong as the next wave engulfed the bow. The sea hammered the ship, dislodging the Tomahawk. The twenty-foot missile tumbled across the deck and slid toward the port side.

On the bridge the CO, along with everyone else, braced against whatever they could.

The officer of the deck ordered, "Helm, get our aft to the wind. Change course bearing two four five."

The young boatswain's mate was already turning, and broke protocol to save time. "Aye sir, changing course bearing two four five."

The captain keyed the squawk box to speak to the FC down in CIC. "Petty officer, this is your captain. Status on that missile."

"Sir, hot ejection completed," came the reply, "But there's been a malfunction. The missile is inactive."

"Hell, I can see that!" the captain yelled. "It's sitting on our damn deck. So, is it completely inert? Or is the turbofan engine going to engage?"

"Sir, this is uncharted territory," said the 2nd Class fire controlman. "They're designed to travel to the target and detonate. And all of that's programmed before we even launch. It should be fine."

The captain growled. "Understood, we might be sitting with a ticking bomb on our deck, but probably not." Without waiting for a reply, he looked to the petty officer of the watch. "Larson get that thing over the side and off my ship."

"Aye, Captain," said the first-class boatswain's mate. He turned and picked up the phone.

The E-4, Petty Officer Third Class Smith, eased his way around the superstructure. The weather decks were restricted access to all but approved personnel. Though the course change put the sudden storm behind them, the sea was still plenty rough.

The young BM3 led four other men, seamen recruits and apprentices from various departments, to the huge cylinder. It sat straight along the section of rails on the port side of the deck. "Careful but quick," Smith said. "And done right the first time. This thing weighs well over a ton. Don't want anyone overboard or injured."

Each man wore a life vest and was tethered to a safety track. They all wore rubber work gloves with texturized palms for extra grip. They had a boom and two slings. The plan was to get the finned tail of the missile over the side, then lift the nose, and let gravity do the rest.

Two men approached the missile just forward of its fins. The fins were keeping that end of the cylinder raised off the deck, allowing room for them to safely pass the sling completely under and around the Tomahawk. Then they ran the sling between the bottom set of deck rails, where they intended the missile to pass. Smith moved the boom so that its arm extended just outside the rails. The men attached the sling from that side, so the boom could pull the Tomahawk away from the ship.

"Okay!" Smith yelled over the waves. "Get clear while I pull its ass end."

He worked the buttons to slightly lift and maneuver the Tomahawk. Soon the tail was angled out over the side of the ship. He was careful not to pull it too far out since the last thing any of them wanted was the sling to hang on the fins and bang the missile against the side. All the while, Smith prayed for the sea to stay calm as possible. Finally, he ordered, "Now position that second one."

Wasting no time, another pair of sailors slipped another sling beneath the Tomahawk, this time keeping the entire thing on their side of the railing. The outer sling was holding the missile slightly aloft, allowing them to again easily slip the reinforced material underneath. They attached this second sling to the boom, right next to the first one, but left its entire length on the inward side of the railing.

Finally, they removed the first sling, careful as the weight shifted and was quickly caught by the second. Again, Smith had them clear out as he worked the boom.

The sling began to lift the forward half. Then, in a sudden movement, the weight passed its tipping point and the missile slid free of the sling, into the ocean. It splashed and sent up a high geyser of water as it dropped away into the depths and was gone.

Satisfied the Tomahawk was safely overboard, Petty Officer Smith ordered his shipmates back inside. "I'll secure this boom," he yelled over the wind, "Get below."

The junior enlisted men moved steadily, but cautiously, back toward the superstructure. Then the sea betrayed them. A swell of water rose and cleared the side. Petty Officer Smith was lifted from his feet and swept toward the rail.

He grabbed with both hands, but the force of the water was too much. Like an unstoppable avalanche it pummeled him, tearing his grip loose and pushing him over the side. He plunged into the water, was swept back against the hull of the ship where he stopped, at last reaching the end of his safety line.

No big deal, he thought, he had on his life vest and the line was secure. His shipmates would pull him back up in no time. Then he saw a fin surface in the pitching sea. Then a scaled monster, there was no other word for it, emerged beneath the fin. Smith's blood ran cold.

It was like an angler fish, only much bigger and more hideous. The thing was the size of a basking shark. Its mouth was a gaping maw of thin, curved teeth. Long and pointed as sabers, the teeth would certainly pierce his flesh and break his bones.

Smith started praying. He jerked on the line, signaling the others to pull him in. He realized then; he was already moving. Already being retrieved. But no way were they going fast enough.

"C'mon, guys! Hurry, dammit!" he screamed, as the beast closed in. "Help me! God help me!"

Its scales were large as silver dollars and protruded from its hide like the armor of an alligator, or some more ancient beast. Smith was being hoisted from the sea, as it closed the remaining distance.

"Nooooooooo!!!"

It flicked a massive tail and surged up from the rolling waves, opened its mouth wide and enveloped Smith in a single gulp. Its jaws snapped shut, severing the line. Immediately the great fish changed direction mid-air and dove back into the briny deep.

"You heard 'em folks," Hank said, releasing the radio switch to break comms with the destroyer. "This just became a rescue mission."

As officer of the deck, Shiv ordered, "Helm. Up on the foils and let's get there."

"Roger that." Belfry worked the controls. "Putting the hammer down and switching to flight mode."

Hank relayed the message to the rest of the crew via intercom then turned to Shiv. "Good job, Petty Officer, but I need you on the charts. I'll take it from here."

"Aye, sir." She moved to the charts and donned a headset, establishing comms to gather data.

"Attention on the bridge," Hank said. "I have the conn."

Everyone acknowledged and kept working.

Soon they were off the water, racing ahead at 45 knots. Belfry grinned, then noticed Hank's somber expression. "Sorry sir. I know some poor squid is bouncing in the waves, but this is fun as hell."

Hank let a smile play briefly at the corners of his mouth. "Never gets old, does it?" Then, just as quickly, he put on his game face. "But let's stay focused. We'll be inside the search grid before we know it. Fleet's gotta stick to their mission, so it's up to us to find him."

At that moment Red stepped onto the bridge. "Any details?"

Shiv had her face in the charts and the headset over one ear. "A Boatswain's Mate," she said without looking up. "He's got a vest on, so at least there's that."

Red said nothing. If the waves grew treacherous enough or an apex predator happened by, a vest wouldn't matter. He moved over near the chart. "Where did he enter the water?"

She pointed to a spot near the top third of the map. "Fell about here, around twenty minutes ago. We're a good half hour out but given the wind speed and waves, he could be anywhere in this sector by the time we get close." She indicated an oval she'd drawn around a red "X". "Like a needle in a haystack, that's what this'll be."

Hank joined them. "Red, get a set of binocs and a rifle."

Red gave a puzzled look. "We expecting a shoot the shark, shoot the man scenario?"

Hank rubbed his chin. "Just got a bad vibe about this whole thing. Want to be ready, is all."

"Yes sir." Red started to leave.

"And have Johnson and Waymore get the big gun ready, just in case."

Red had the door open and a hand on the frame. He turned back toward Hank. "Think we'll need the harpoons?"

Hank hesitated. "I'm hoping I'm just paranoid. Let's stick to rifles and the 62 cal for now. And put on a life vest."

"Understood." Red stepped out and dogged the door behind.

Chapter 24

January 17, 1991
The Red Sea
0700 hours

They reached the perimeter of Shiv's search oval during a lull in the storm. Hank ordered the Scorpius hull borne at 10 knots so they could begin their search pattern.

Red was on the starboard side, just aft of the bridge, with a M16A2 slung across one shoulder and a set of binoculars strapped around his neck. He let the binocs hang against his life vest as he scanned the ocean with the Mark I eyeball.

The door opened behind him, but Red didn't look. Instead, he kept his eyes to the waves.

"I've got Duncan on the port side," said Hank from behind. "Just picked up the fleet at the edge of our radar. Looks like they're still raining death on Baghdad."

"Good," Red muttered. His skin pricked as every hair stood on end.

"What the hell?" Hank whispered. "You feel that?"

"Like someone just walked across my grave. Hank, there's something otherworldly in this water."

"I'm gonna check on Dunc. You be careful."

Red nodded. He brought his binoculars up.

Hank was halfway around, walking behind the bridge, between it and the Mk-140 Harpoon launchers, when the water on the port side swelled. Red dropped his binocs and grabbed the cable to keep his footing. He turned and saw the swell open like it was about to heave lunch on their deck.

"Might be a good time to shoulder that weapon!" Hank shouted.

Red saw the creature leap and clear the rail. Arcs of water trailed behind it.

Hank ducked.

But it wasn't enough. The fish clamped down on his arm, mid-leap. But its trajectory was thrown off by the harpoon assembly, which caught the monster's tail and turned the beast sideways. It flopped to the deck, hanging tightly to Hank.

Red unsnapped a sheath on his belt and pulled a long knife.

The scaled monster arched on its tail, flipping itself against the Harpoons, this time with enough force to rip the Mk-140 launchers from the deck. The *Scorpius* rocked. Red stumbled but didn't fall.

Thrashing again, the fish slammed into the weapons and sent them skidding across the fantail. For a moment, the launchers teetered on the edge of the stern, then dumped over the side — both quad assembly Mk-140 launchers, fully loaded, for a total of eight RGM-84 Harpoons, lost.

Red brought his rifle to bear, the knife in his other hand as he charged, determined to save Hank.

The floundering creature flipped again, clearing the rails to splash into the sea, pulling Hank over with it.

"Nooo!" Red scanned the water frantically. He saw nothing but a churning whirlpool. His mind raced. With Hank's life on the line, no way they'd bring the 62 cal into play.

Then he saw the creature surface not five feet from the *Scorpius*, still dragging Hank — as if toying with the man. Without a second thought, Red slipped between the cables, waited for his moment, then jumped.

Red landed in a crouched position right beside the creature's main fin. He drove his blade deep into the flesh, between plates of armored scale. He held on as the fish leapt high into the air and released Hank.

Red pressed the business end of his M-16 into a spot just behind the head, angling toward what he hoped was the brain. The fish pounded the waves in a violent splashdown. He squeezed the trigger, delivering a spray of rounds into the beast, like a bang stick to the back of a gator's skull. But with three quick doses of lead instead of a single shot.

The scaled monstrosity twitched, jerking its tail involuntarily from side to side in a death seizure. Red still held on. Finally, the creature's muscles clenched in paralysis. Then it trembled in one last spasm as water engulfed them. Red held tight to the knife handle, his anchor point, as the beast went limp and started to drift into a slow turn, sinking.

Red glimpsed Dunc on the port rail. "Get Hank out of the water!"

"We're pulling him in now!" Dunc pointed aftward.

The sea had swallowed Red's knees. "Then throw me a line!"

Dunc gave a puzzled look, then shrugged and took a line from the bulkhead. He tossed it out.

Red finally let go of his knife, leaving it in the fish. He tied the line to his M16, then started shucking his life vest.

"What the hell are you doing?" Dunc shouted.

Red swam free with his tethered weapon in one hand. He dove straight down, pushing past the giant fish, then looped under it as it continued to sink. He found the gill next to its right pectoral fin and shoved his M-16 deep into the frilled layers of bright pink flesh. He turned it sideways to lodge it in place, effectively hooking the beast.

He pushed away and clawed back to the surface with two strokes. Breaching, he yelled, "Secure that line! We're hauling this bastard in!"

On his swim back, Red snagged his life vest then clambered up onto the aft deck. He called to Duncan, who was securing the line around a cleat. "We're gonna need a boom," Red told him, as the younger man reached a hand to help him up and to his feet. "How's Hank?"

Dunc faltered. "Doc's got a tourniquet on his arm. That's all I know."

In the absence of their CO, Red took charge of the junior serviceman. "Keep an eye on this thing. I'm gonna check on our captain."

Dunc nodded absently, his face pale and eyes wide. Red realized in that moment just how young the man was. No matter what he'd seen or experienced to get an offer to join 13, Duncan was still a teenager.

"It's gonna be alright," Red assured him.

"Just worried about Hank, is all."

Red put a hand on his shoulder. "*You* go check on him. I can set up the winch."

The younger man looked at him with gratitude. "Thanks, Red. Yeah, I'll let you know when I get back."

"No hurry." Red set to work so Dunc could go.

The young man wasted no time, and neither did Red. In short order the line was mated to a motorized winch at the end of a sturdy adjustable arm.

Red was holding down the button on the boom's control box when Duncan returned, with Waymore beside him this time. Reaching with a wharfing hook to pull the beast onto the deck, Red ventured, "Good news, I hope."

"Cap's a tough SOB," said Waymore, "But he's gonna lose that arm."

Red frowned but kept his eyes on his work. "Is he awake at all?" More than anything, Red had worried about blood loss and shock.

"Yeah," answered Dunc. "Told us to get our asses out here and help you."

The fish was positioned over the empty spot where the launcher had been. So, there was plenty of room as Red depressed another button to lower it to the deck.

"Well then, you guys get some lines over this bad boy and let's strap him down tight."

"That is one ugly mug," said Waymore, as Dunc hurried to get the lines.

Red finished winching it down. "Like an angler and a basking shark had a baby." He went over to pry the rifle back out of its gills.

"Look at the jaws on this thing." Waymore took a line from Dunc and started lashing it to eye.

"Careful," Red warned, finally wrenching his M-16 free. "Could be poison in those teeth, even in the fins. The less contact with this thing, the better." He stood and started to untie his soaked weapon.

"Damn thing's not dead!" Waymore yelled, jerking his pistol and taking aim at the forehead.

Dunc followed suit, pulling his sidearm.

"Hold your fire!" Red shouted. He held up a hand. "I see it too, guys. Be ready, but don't fire unless you have to. Especially this close to the ship."

Waymore gave a hurried reply, "Ain't gonna hit the deck or ricochet into somebody. Just wanna put another round in its head."

"Head ain't moving." Red stepped over and jerked his knife from where he'd planted it in the thing's back. "Matter of fact, only thing moving is its belly."

Waymore started to calm, aware now the midsection was expanding and contracting in a very irregular fashion. It wasn't movement by the fish, not even a desperate attempt at breathing. The thing's eyes were fixed in death, its body limp except for that roiling motion beneath the scales of its belly.

"You are bat-shit crazy," said Dunc, keeping his weapon trained on the fish's head.

"Nope," Red replied, "That honorific belongs to Belfry. What *I* am is highly versatile." He plunged the blade into a spot anterior to the movement, then carefully began to slice a jagged line between the scales, slicing forward and running just under the dorsal fin.

Finally, he had a flap of skin peeled away. He reached in and took hold of the fish's belly. In response the gut sac started writhing in earnest.

"Hold still!" Red yelled, "I'm trying to help you!"

As if something inside understood, the movement settled. Red resumed, inserting the knife carefully and cutting an opening near what had to be the top.

A sudden splash of liquid spilled out, but there was also air, rancid and foul smelling. The stomach deflated, settling close around a crouched form. Like a fetus curled inside a womb.

Red began to cut more feverishly. "Keep those guns ready, but don't shoot unless you have to, and be ready to help me."

"What the hell..." Dunc whispered, as the opening widened.

Red slashed in a ninety-degree turn. He lifted away one side of the stomach to finally expose the contents.

"I'll be..." muttered Waymore. He holstered his weapon and moved to help Red. "Dunc, you finish tying this thing down while we carry this poor soul to Doc."

"He's alive." Red gently cradled the man's torso while Waymore picked up his legs. They carefully carried the ragged man away from the beast and toward the bridge.

With eyes still wide and face pale as ever, Dunc worked furiously. He tied the fish tighter than necessary, so he could hurry up and join the others.

Chapter 25

January 17, 1991
The Red Sea
0700 hours

Saxüru had been patrolling the sea, his head above water as he swam, when the humans unleashed their sky weapons. Their huge, metal clad spears sped fast and high, thrown to the northeastern sky only to disappear beyond the shore. Obviously, these humans had targeted some far away enemy upon the land. He stared after the volley, wondering at their destination. Could it be Babylon, at war again even after these many centuries? The trajectory made it plausible.

The demigod had promptly submerged and swam toward the fissure which alarmed his underlings, those wretched spawn of Dagon. Saxüru felt the tremors when the weapons finally found their target. Even at a great distance, the seabed trembled. With the ensuing destruction, the fissure between realms widened just enough for the great fish to finally ram its way through.

Saxüru had watched as Dendan ascended. In that same moment, Saxüru's merfolk showed the extent of their cowardice and the limits to their loyalty. Instead of standing by their master, they fled.

Saxüru let them go, content to be rid of them... for the moment. There would still be a time of reckoning.

He called a dozen sharks to his side. Positioned himself in their center. Floating in their midst, he watched as Dendan swam past.

Released by the deadly strike, Dendan was also drawn to those who delivered it. The great fish paid Saxüru no mind, as it sped from the depths to churn the waters and begin exacting payment in lieu of the sacrifice that should have been made. The beast was a war-god, after all, and was due his tribute as such.

Saxüru followed, the circle of sharks keeping pace, held in thrall by their master. He watched as the tossing sea accomplished what sailors of old would have done instinctively. In ancient times a sacrifice would have been cast over the side. In this age, Dendan was forced to take what was his.

Saxüru marveled at humanity's ignorance, appalled by the extent of lost knowledge. When it came to the gods, they had abandoned so much. Still, though they were ignorant, Saxüru was mesmerized by their tenacity. Though not an effortless defeat, the relatively quick demise of Dendan came as a surprise.

It occurred to Saxüru, as he watched the scaled corpse being pulled from the sea, that his plan for using the great fish to lure the humans into an alliance had been hastily made. Not to mention a vast underestimation on his part.

No matter, he decided, with each encounter he learned that much more.

He grimaced. So much for the beast which had terrified his cowardly Merfolk. Now they would know true fear.

As would the humans. For it was apparent now that this generation of humans was quite different than those he once ruled.

Loathe as he was to admit it, Saxüru recognized the fact that a war to subdue them would be costly indeed. He would need one of the fiercest of his chattel for the task.

The Serpent.

But it would take time to summon the creature. And great effort to keep it under his will. Saxüru would need all his strength, would need a steady increase in tensions and bloodshed to feed upon, so that the beast could be awakened from the great trench where it had slumbered for hundreds of years.

With a gesture he dismissed the sharks. They dispersed in a dozen directions. Saxüru made his way to his throne upon the ridge. He needed to be alone so he could devise a plan and set it in motion. There was, after all, a kingdom to reclaim.

Chapter 26

The Red Sea
January 17, 1991
0710 hours

As they carried the man, Red couldn't help but feel he recognized this sailor. He couldn't afford more than a glance, and the face was pale, slick with mucus, obscured by scraps of half-eaten kelp. A life vest was in place, covering the man's uniform, with dog tags surely buried under that.

They made it to the bridge where Doc came out to greet them. "Let me check him here, before we move him below."

Waymore and Red set him gently on the deck. Duncan caught up and knelt with them.

For the second time that day, Doc set to work saving a life and, beyond that, salvaging as much of that life as possible. First, he removed the vest, checked the breathing and pulse, looked for any signs of injury, blood, compound fractures, then felt for broken bones. "This is one lucky son of a gun," he said, as he used a damp cloth to start cleaning the man.

Red looked at the blue work shirt. Stenciled above the left pocket was the name Smith. He whispered tentatively, "Smitty?"

"Let's see if you've got a first name." Doc pulled out the tags and read, "Dale Smith."

Red's jaw dropped. "Smitty!" He repositioned himself and took the man's face in his hands. "Holy crap, it *is* you."

"Okay guys, get ready," said Doc. "I had to put the captain to sleep, but let's see if I can wake our modern-day Jonah." He looked at the other men. "Hold him. With what he's endured and probably seen, he may come out swinging."

Waymore asked, "Should we tie him down first?"

"Not tying him down." Red frowned. "In case y'all couldn't tell, I know this man. Just let me be the first one he sees."

"Sure," said Doc. "Suit yourself. You guys just hold tight. Dunc, get in here. The more the merrier."

Duncan put a hand on Smitty's left shoulder.

Doc gave a final glance around. "Here we go." He held the salt capsule close to Smith's face and popped it open.

Smitty snapped awake. His body tensed for a moment as he shook his head in response to the chemicals. He blinked and coughed, then stared at the face before him. "Red?" he asked, and his body relaxed.

All the men slowly released their hold. Red grinned. "Hey Smitty. How you feeling, bud?"

Smitty coughed. "I reckon it's how a cricket feels." He gave a weak smile. "You know, after it's had a hook shoved up its ass, then swallowed by a bluegill."

Red gave a small chuckle.

"You're one tough squid," said Waymore.

Smitty raised an eyebrow. "Thanks?" He looked to Red again. "Got my stripe—BM3. Can't help but think you had something to do with it. I know I bombed that test."

Red swallowed hard. "It's good to see you, bro." He touched Smitty's shoulder. "We're gonna help you get cleaned up. Then you get some rest."

"And after that, the questions," said Smitty.

Red shrugged. "You know the drill."

Smitty gave him a sly glance. "Got a few questions myself."

Red nodded. "Of course. I owe you some answers."

"Don't owe me nothing. Just wanna catch up, is all."

Doc spoke up. "Right. Let's get you out of this slime suit and into something clean. C'mon guys…" he looked around. "Let's move him below."

Hank was unconscious, sedated and resting while the *Scorpius* made its way back to Lemonnier. They would, of course, transfer the fish to an outbound cargo ship. Arrangements were made and the brass at Quantico were anxious to receive the prize.

Belfry was about Smitty's size, so he gave him an unmarked set of dungarees. After a long, deep sleep, Smitty awoke ravenous. He answered their questions the best he could.

From what they could tell, given Doc's assessment and Smitty's account, the creature had swallowed him whole. Curling into a ball as he slid past the fangs had probably saved him from being shot full of venom. The fact that the fish swallowed a huge gulp of air was another lucky break.

As near as they could calculate, he was in the thing's belly for almost an hour. Again, the vest and outer garments had protected him from the stomach acids. Doc also theorized the acids were relatively weak. Its fangs were designed to inject a venom that would soften him up from the inside. Much like a spider, the fish's prey was digested by venom. Then, instead of sucking out the juice as a spider would, the great fish would simply rely on the prey to break down until its entire composition was that of a soupy mass of nutrients. Since Smitty was never bitten, decomposition never began.

The swallowed air had been enough to sustain him during the ordeal. He was nearing the end of his supply when they found him—the reason he was still moving and then abruptly went unconscious. He hadn't heard Red's order to 'hold still', he'd simply passed out from lack of oxygen. From all indications, they'd found him in the nick of time.

"And you didn't panic," Red pointed out. "Seem to be in a stable frame of mind. Reckon the higher ups might wanna have a talk with you."

"About what?"

"Joining up, what else?"

"If you'll recall, me and Ortiz ran like hell when that Banshee appeared."

"Any nightmares after that?"

"Nope?"

"Daydreams, then? Looking over your shoulder, especially when you're near a graveyard?"

"Don't exactly hang out in graveyards, Red. Besides, let's leave this psycho anal-ness to the guys in shades and shiny shoes."

Red laughed. "Y'know, Smitty, all things considered, I think you're gonna be just fine." He grew serious again. "But I need to catch up on the captain."

They were up on the foils at Doc's urging, but still a few hours from Lemonnier, when Red entered Doc's makeshift sickbay. He walked in, expecting to see Hank quietly resting. Instead, the man was awake, breathing laboriously. One arm was gone from the shoulder down. That side heavily bandaged. Doc was on a stool at his side.

"Cap?" Red started. "Just wanted to check on you."

Both men looked over. The expression on Doc's face said it all.

"C'mere," Hank managed with a wheeze.

Doc protested quietly, "Sir, you need your rest."

"Dammit." Hank fixed Red with a determined gaze, then motioned with his good hand. "Get...over here."

Red moved closer, trying to keep his presence from being an intrusion. "Doc is right, sir. You need to rest." But he didn't move away, sensing the inevitable.

"Poison took my arm," Hank managed, "Doc did his best to amputate in time, but..." He paused, took a ragged, shallow breath, then said, "...but it's in my chest. Can't exactly feel much. But I'm dying. And it can't be stopped." He looked to Doc. "Did your best. As much as anyone could've. And I appreciate that." Hank turned his eyes to Red. "Make sure everyone knows..." He coughed, wheezed. "Knows how much I ..." A tear ran down his cheek as he reached with his one, trembling hand.

"Absolutely, Cap." Red took his hand. "And the feeling's mutual. I speak for everyone on that."

"You've got command now," Hank replied, in barely a whisper. "Take 'em on home. And look in my locker. Divvy up my stuff among the crew. You get the black shirt ... the one with that 13 patch. Hell, you earned it...long ago."

Red mumbled through his tears, "Hang in there, Hank. *Fight* it."

Hank looked back to Doc. "Make sure they know... that I put this knucklehead in charge. Do that for me, Doc."

The young man nodded. "Sure thing, sir." He ignored the tears running down his own face. "And I'll make sure *you* get home."

Hank Grimson turned his eyes one last time to Red. "Heard you killed the fish. Thanks for making that thing pay."

"Gonna make that goat-headed thing pay, too. That's who's behind this."

"And when you see Cassie again..." Hank coughed. "Give her a hug for me. Tell her ... tell her she was...like the little sister I never wanted."

Red gave a wan smile. "You've got it, Hank."

The man smiled back, weakly. "And you...were the red-headed step-brother." He motioned Red closer. "Got something to say ... just for you."

Red leaned in so Hank could whisper in his ear.

"Be good to her, Red."

He pulled back and said, "Hank. I..." Then he noticed Hank's breathing had stopped. His eyes didn't move.

Doc reached over and carefully closed their captain's eyes.

Chapter 27

January 17, 1991
The Red Sea

Under cloak of darkness, Saxüru left the Sea. Swimming into the shallows and then clawing his way onto the shore, his transformation began.

First, he took in great gulps of air, causing his gills to seal shut along his jaw line as his lungs adapted to accept their new source of oxygen. Then the scales retracted into his skin as his pigment shifted to match that of the local humans.

A great beard sprouted and flowed to his chest. His tail split down the middle, morphing into the jointed limbs of a biped. Upon his scalp, a jagged scar marked the site of his broken horn. The only things which remained unchanged were those piercing, golden eyes.

He took the staff from where he kept it, slung across his back. Slipped the camel-hide sack from a shoulder and reached inside. Within moments he wore the loose attire of a desert nomad.

Saxüru cast a glance toward the waters. Though he could no longer see their vessels, he knew the ones who had slain Dendan were still there. Felt in his heart that he would face them someday in battle.

He raised his staff and held it outstretched toward the sea. A desert breeze wandered by and lifted the folds of his garment, billowing the sleeves to complete the striking image of an old Bedouin wizard casting his spell.

But he was far more than that, more even than the most powerful djinn. Saxüru was of the Ancients. He cast his senses upon the drifting seaward wind, then felt an answer as vibrations from far away reached back. A great battle lay ahead. One more brutal, more deadly, more deliciously destructive than any blood feast he had ever known.

He breathed in the salt air a final time before departure. Then turned his face to the ancient city of Babylon and began the long, northeastern trek. It was time to prepare. Set his pieces in place and begin the game.

Smitty was recruited into JTF13. Even though Red had mentioned the possibility, the offer was still a surprise to Smitty. But not to Red, nor the rest of the crew for that matter. Smith was sent to the indoctrination course and then whatever duty station suited the brass.

Hank's body was sent back home for burial. The crew of the *Scorpius* had to stay at Lemonnier, so they held a memorial service for him. There were lots of tears, sea stories, and even a few laughs. Belfry had restrung a battered acoustic guitar and led them all in a surprisingly beautiful rendition of 'Amazing Grace'. But in the end, it was the turning point from which the crew, as it had been, would never recover. And though no one else seemed to blame him, Red couldn't help but think he was at least in some small way responsible. Still, he managed to push those feelings aside and soldier on.

The remainder of 1991 was spent mostly in support of the conventional troops since a presence in the region was maintained.

The crew got a new captain, a Navy lieutenant named Sheffield, originally from Alaska and recruited after some run-in off the coast of Japan. Other than that, the year seemed uneventful to Red, like a vague period of mourning that he waded through. Then the crew was rotated, and Red was sent to Intel Headquarters. It was there, behind a desk instead of a deck railing, that life got interesting again.

John S. Worth

Chapter 28

January 13, 1992
Quantico, JTF 13 Headquarters
0650 hours

Red slid behind the desk with a sense of foreboding. But maybe it was for the best. Maybe desk duty was what he deserved, payment for what happened to Hank. His own personal Hell, or at least purgatory, for everything he'd done or failed to do.

He booted the computer and logged on.

A knock came at his door. Red turned to see a familiar face.

"Cassie!" He grinned and stood back up. Offered a hand.

She hesitated, then set a blue paper bag on the floor and awkwardly shook his outstretched right with her left.

He turned red. "Oh hell, I forgot."

She laughed it off. "Which only proves you don't think of me as that one-armed female officer. That is…if you ever do think of me."

"Of course I think of you. I just...." He faltered.

Cassie laughed louder. "You're turning even more red." Then she let him off the hook. "It's great to see you,

Tom. Welcome to Beulah Land." She glanced around at the bare walls. "Guess you're just settling in?"

"First day," he admitted. Then he sighed. "I reckon you heard about Hank."

She looked away. "I read the report. He was a good man. A great friend. It sounded a lot like what happened to me. What could've happened." She bent to the bag. "I've got something for you," she said, as if eager to change the subject. She handed it to him.

He gave a quizzical look, reached in, and took out a 16 x 20 matted photo. It was the picture she'd taken the day she left, of the *Scorpius* and her crew. There was Hank mugging with his two favorite knuckleheads. And Red, fresh to the crew, standing at the other end of the line.

"It's…." Red swallowed hard. It took a moment to compose himself. "It's damn beautiful. is what it is."

Cassie smiled. "You're welcome." She glanced at her watch. "I've got a meeting coming up. but was wondering if you're free for lunch."

His mood lifted. "Yeah. That would be nice."

"Great. If memory serves, it's my turn to foot the bill."

He shrugged. "Absolutely. So, are you gonna swing by here, or…?"

"11:45," she said. "I'll meet you out front, show you my favorite cafe."

He smiled. "See you then."

She returned the smile, gave a short nod and was gone.

Red watched her go, then sat down to his computer and realized he was still smiling.

Maybe a desk job wasn't purgatory after all.

Over lunch, Red pressed in with, "I never got a chance to ask. How'd you get invited to join 13?"

"I can't tell you everything since most of the details are need-to-know classified, but basically I kind of stumbled into it."

"Don't we all?"

"Well, mine was more a case of finding something no one else saw. When I brought it to my chain of command, I was taken off that assignment and told to forget about it."

"Only you didn't?"

"Oh, I completely did. But then it happened again, with an entirely different set of data. That's when I was basically accused of hacking when all I'd done was recognize patterns."

"So, this time they saw your potential..."

"You'd think so. But I was reassigned *again*. A month later I connected the dots between some field skirmishes and chatter among the local residents of a third world country. I think it was a combination of chauvinism and arrogance that kept blinding my higher ups to what was going on."

"So, you paid attention to stories about sea monsters and such, and saw correlation between skirmishes and supernatural activity?"

"Absolutely. Instead of dismissing folklore and rumor out of hand, I'd look at it first. Most of the time it was nothing, but after a while you kind of develop a knack for sorting the reliable from the rubbish. At least I did."

"And someone finally listened to you?"

"Of course not. I got my third reassignment and a reprimand in my record. At which point I filed a formal complaint."

"Discrimination?"

"Damn straight. If a male officer had connected those dots, he'd be hailed a wunderkind. This was back in '87. I told them their good-old-boys club mentality was going to get soldiers killed. They were missing patterns left and right and trying to penalize me for seeing what they couldn't."

"How long did that complaint drag on?"

"Barely even got started. But it got *someone's* attention. A recruiter from 13 waltzed in and put a stop to it by making me an offer. Then the chain of command was restructured so that, hopefully, it wouldn't happen again. My reprimand was removed, and I was given the choice of my next command. That's when I joined the crew of the *Scorpius*."

"Any particular reason for that?"

"Without going into those details I mentioned, let's just say everything I'd stumbled upon was tied to that region. I just wanted a closer look. I started sending out my probes and listening in on local scuttlebutt. I'd still be there if Morrison hadn't wanted me here."

"Good thing he did," Red pointed out. "You wouldn't have gotten that wound taken care of in time on the *Scorpius*. Good as Doc is, he wouldn't have been fast enough."

"How is the crew?" she asked.

Red shrugged. "After the Dendan incident everything sort of...changed. But all in all, they were doing fine when I left. By now most of 'em have rotated anyway."

She smiled at him. "Your turn."

Red started with the day he rang the bell.

John S. Worth

Chapter 29

July 16, 1992
Quantico, Virginia
1845 hours

Though Red never would've guessed it, life at Intel quickly became as thrilling as his days at sea. His first lunch with Cassie led to another, then became a weekly occurrence, which spilled into the weekends, and by mid-July led them to a crossroad.

"Tom, what are we doing?" she asked, her head on his shoulder as they watched 'Star Trek TNG' in her apartment.

"Not sure about you, but I was just thinking how glad I am this spinoff made it past three seasons."

"You know that's not what I mean."

He kissed the top of her head. "I'm enjoying time with my favorite person in the world. Hoping it never ends."

She sat up straight, grabbed the remote from the coffee table and clicked off the set. Her brows lowered as she turned to him. "Don't say things you don't mean." Before he could reply she stood and said, "I'll be thirty this year. I know it's only been six months, but if this isn't going anywhere, I'd rather know sooner than later."

Red stalled. "I'm just glad we're not in trouble for fraternizing."

At that her eyes narrowed. "Fraternization be damned," she said. "You don't work for me. And besides that, being a part of the Task Force better have some privileges." Then she composed herself, but there was still the hint of tears in her voice as she said, "But that's beside the point and you know it. Now answer my question, Tom."

He sighed. "Do we really have to do this now?" He gestured to her television. "Geordi just got the warp core online and Picard's about to engage."

"Seriously?" Her face went blank. "I can't believe—"

With a loud groan, Red stopped her mid-sentence. He slipped from the couch and stretched out on the floor, putting an arm around her legs. He stared up with pleading eyes. "Just a little later. After this episode. We can ride out to the beach, take a walk—"

She put her hand on her hip. "Tom, I'm trying to talk about us. Our future, if there is one." Her lips began to tremble. "You'd better take this seriously or I'm going to ask you to—"

"Guess Picard's got the right idea." He sighed again and started to get up, moving to a crouched position. He pulled his other hand into view. "I wanted to do this on the beach, under the stars. But you and that damn Jean Luc...."

Cassie was dumbstruck. She finally realized he was on one knee, was gently taking hold of her hand, and held in his other a small open case. Rose colored velvet on the outside, pink satin within, and there in the middle a thin, gold band, filigreed all around, with what had to be a ¾ carat in a delicate setting.

"Will you make me the happiest man alive? Cassandra Straub, sweet love of my heart, precious woman my soul yearns for, will you marry me?"

Red looked to Cassie with a sly smile as they walked along the beach. Cassie smiled then asked, "How long have you been planning that?"

"The idea first crossed my mind on September 15, 1990."

"When you boarded the *Scorpius*?"

"The moment I saw you."

John S. Worth

Chapter 30

December 14, 1992
Quantico, JTF 13 Headquarters
0700 hours

First thing on a Monday morning, Red was called into Morrison's office. The door was open, so he poked his head in. "You wanted to see me sir?" he asked.

Morrison finished typing at his computer, then said, "Sure. Have a seat, Red." He motioned to a nearby seat. The office was austere, with a simple desk pushed against the wall. The computer was angled so no one but Morrison could see the screen. There was a college diploma on the wall and a few certificates. But nothing garish, and no huge desk separating the two men, or other signs that Morrison was concerned with setting up an image of hierarchy. "Just want to run something by you," he said. "See what you think before I bring anyone else in."

He pulled an 8 x 10 from his briefcase. "This is one of two copies of this photo. I've got the original, which I developed myself, and the film." He passed it over. "Ever seen this guy?"

Before it even got to him, the shape of a tall figure fired neurons in Red's memory. "Yeah," he said. "But just once. On the shore of Eretria. Put a chill down my spine, and I've never forgotten him." He shook his head, taking in the photo. There in the close-up, talking with locals in what seemed to be an Iraqi village was the Bedouin wizard, beard, robe, sack, and staff. Just like Red remembered. "I thought he was a mirage. So, do we have a name for this mystery man?"

"We're working on that," said Morrison. "But there's not much to go on. Was wondering if you could help."

Red furrowed his brow. "That staff," he said. "I didn't realize it at the time. But damned if it doesn't look the same."

"Same as what?"

Red looked Morrison in the eyes. "As the staff Saxüru was holding when he rode in on that crocodile." Red nodded slowly. "And that sack. See that bulge there?" He pointed at the curved shape pushing against the fabric of the pack slung over the Bedouin's shoulder.

"Like a horn," Morrison noted.

"Pretty sure the report we submitted had a description of Saxüru. Of course, we got no photos, but..."

"One horned," Morrison said. "Your report showed an attention to detail that impressed me." He smiled. "Here we are years later, and it pays off."

"So, you think this wizard is connected to Saxüru."

"He's carrying around a horn, shaped like the one missing on the water god the *Scorpius* battled. What do you think?"

"I think it is Saxüru," Red answered. "And look at that scar." He pointed to a place on the man's forehead, just visible below the edge of the scarf wrapped around a head of thinning hair. "Probably lends him a certain credence in the eyes of the ones he's trying to influence."

"A shape-shifter." Morrison steepled his fingers and leaned back in his chair. "Red, keep this to yourself for now. I'll bring in Cassie, of course, get her to start gathering intel. Until we know more, I'd rather not divert resources."

Though he didn't entirely agree or understand, Red had learned to trust Morrison's judgment. "Yes sir. Will that be all?"

"Just for one more thing." He took the photo and put it away. "Helen called Cassie last night. You two are coming over for supper on Thursday. Just a heads up."

Red smiled, as he stood to go. "Gotcha. I'll bring the scotch."

"Single grain," said Morrison, "Not that cheap blended stuff."

"21 year." Red gave a sly wink. He walked out, leaving the door open.

Chapter 31

January 9, 1993
Quantico, Virginia
2230 hours

Having quietly slipped from their reception, Red and Cassie began undressing in their hotel suite. A morning flight would usher them to Cancun for a week, but first they intended to enjoy the last few hours of their day before getting some much-needed rest.

Red put the rented black tuxedo coat aside and loosened his bow tie. He started back on the conversation he'd begun in the limo, "All I'm saying is that, for once. I'd like to be preemptive."

Cassie frowned and set her veil gently on a dresser.

He unbuttoned his white shirt and continued, "I mean, you've given them all that data. Basically, spelled it out for everyone, and we still have to wait until someone else makes the first move."

"Mm-hmm," Cassie said, she slipped off her shoes and started removing the wedding dress. "I feel just as frustrated and impatient, but you're simply too aggressive, Tom."

"Could be no one else is aggressive enough."

Cassie grinned, setting the dress aside. "Seems like you should've been a Marine and kept to the front lines. Or are we finally talking about a different type of aggression? You ready to make that first move?"

He smiled as he took out the cuff links and slipped free of his shirt. "You really think I should've been a jarhead?" He removed his shoes and then his slacks.

"No." She gave a coy glance. "Wouldn't have found your way to me if you had. And this is where you belong." She removed her bra and pulled him close.

He kissed her then, long and passionately. But afterwards he walked to the closet and hung up his tux. "So, until we respond to the threats brewing and the seeds our friend Saxüru keeps sowing, what are we supposed to do? Just sit on our thumbs?"

She feigned a scowl. They were both aware he was teasing her. "Is that your idea of pillow talk? We keep doing our duty and living our lives. That's what we do." She kicked her stockings to a corner, completely naked now. Her voice dropped low and sultry. "Forget Saxüru. You're the one with seed to sow. So do your duty and get over here. That's an order."

Red swallowed hard. He cleared his throat. "Yes ma'am."

The rest of the decade saw one skirmish after another. Starting in the year they got married. There was plenty of unrest that year. Red kept a log, as he and Cassie continued to pour through intel and gather data.

And though they did get on with the business of doing their duty and living their lives, through the entire simmering decade, Red felt a common thread, an unseen ominous hand pulling the strings. Someone who spoke with a forked tongue, slipping from sea to sand, whispering promises and lies like the serpent he was. Stirring things up so that conflict never settled for long.

Like the memory of a rising plume of smoke, Red sensed something dark on the horizon.

Part Three: Restitution

John S. Worth

Chapter 32

January 17, 1993
The Red Sea

Over time the chasm had widened, but never enough for the great serpent to pass. Then came a shockwave larger than any of the previous ones, obviously closer to the prison in which the gargantuan beast was held. Finally, after eons, it sensed an opening and carefully slipped through.

At first it wandered in cautious trepidation. Indeed, its confines were so ingrained it could scarcely bring itself to swim any pattern of greater reach than the circling trek to which it was accustomed.

Slowly however, with the passing tides it ventured further out in ever-widening circles, but still not daring to rise from the comforting darkness of the cold abyss. Then it came upon a shark. Instinctively it lashed out, feasted again on the flesh of this realm, and began to remember.

Old, forgotten images returned in snatches of vivid detail, followed by brief scenes. How it once raced through the waters, fearing nothing while setting all others to flight with but a glance. It recalled the taste of the scaled and smooth, the finned and tentacled denizen of the deep.

But not only that.

It also remembered those small, thin-skinned creatures who dared venture into domains not their own. Trespassing in strange wooden baskets, they struck out across the surface of the serpent's territory. And, more often than not, paid the ultimate price for their transgressions.

The snake felt again the surge of strength with which it crushed them. How it swiftly coiled around their bundles of sticks to crack them open, spilling those dust-born vermin in a panicked mass of writhing flesh.

It remembered their screams, their useless flailing, and especially the feel of their blood coating its throat, warm and delicious...as salty as the sea.

The great serpent once more grew bolder. Daring to venture to the surface, it found them again, in small vessels, casting nets into the water to catch the silver, swiftly darting fish that roamed the waters.

It attacked them again, for the first time in millennia, as they floated upon the waves like insects on a leaf. Taking one small clutch after another it discreetly snatched them under. Remembering and relishing the taste.

Still, it kept to the smaller vessels, hiding itself from the larger ones which floated gray as clouds across the surface. The serpent was careful not to overreach until it had a better sense of its place in this new world. For this too it remembered: things could change very quickly.

And so, the serpent was cautious and calculating—and waiting for something it could not quite recall. A sound. A signal or calling of some sort.

A summoning.

Saxüru learned much during his time among humans. Their religions remained a source of conflict and killing, and that served his purposes well, although it infuriated him that descendants of the ancient Hebrews still existed. That tribe had been more trouble than any others. He still recalled how the waters of his domain were violated during their escape from Mitzrayim, now known as Egypt. He hated those particular humans, and especially their god, with a vengeance.

Though relations between himself and other demigods, such as Gurax, were tenuous, there was often room for alliances. With that accursed YHWH there was no such thing as compromise. That One wanted humans for himself alone and was impossible to predict or understand.

With Gurax it had been easy: appeal to the creature's pride and appease him with human adoration and fear.

Second-hand worship though it may be, it kept the fish-man sated. Not so with that ancient Hebrew deity.

Another most puzzling entity was the relative newcomer, Allah. Though Saxüru had yet to encounter the god directly, his influence was everywhere. Saxüru spent the first few years in human guise in search of the elusive god. He found nothing but man-made monuments amid a disjointed, though numerous, array of followers. Like adherents to any religion, there were various schisms which had led to many sects, which also led to followers who differed in the degree of their devotion or militancy. The most radical of these fell into his hands easily.

He began to make his rounds, never promoting himself. At least not yet. But steadily Saxüru used his powers of influence to nudge this one and then that into positions of power all around what the rest of the world now called the Middle East.

To him it was the cradle of human civilization. The domain of the ancient ones, among whom he would once again reign supreme. In due time, of course. First, he slowly and methodically positioned all of his pieces upon the boards, then waited for the opportune time.

He began pushing pieces, moving pawns about, drawing them all ever deeper into conflict. Hundreds of thousands died. More would follow. The years passed, the death toll rose, his power grew. Until finally, the conflict began to spill over, drawing in tribes from far away. It was delicious. It was terrible.

It also played into a larger plan. The one he dared not share with anyone. For every master was also a slave, and Saxüru was bound to Numma — the great Goddess of the oceans, a chaotic, creative force without equal. Though he fed on the life force of slain humans, it was ultimately Numma from which he drew his dark, supernatural powers, to achieve the higher purpose of summoning her once again, fully into this realm. And when that happened, she had assured him, Saxüru would indeed reign at her side.

And then the humans delivered a blow that shook the foundations of his sea. Another barrier was breached, and Saxüru sensed the return of one of his most powerful minions. He turned his face and began walking resolutely toward his sea.

Chapter 33

October 12, 2000
Quantico, Virginia
2010 hours

In autumn of the year 2000, Lieutenant Commander Morrison announced his retirement and left Red to finish out his stint at Quantico with Lieutenant Rick Collins, a bespectacled man about Red's age and fresh out of JTF's advanced course.

The man put in long hours and expected the same. Chief Thomas McCraith was preparing to leave after a very long day when he was handed the telegram that signaled the beginning of his most difficult assignment yet.

19:55, October 12, 2000
Quantico, JTF13 Intelligence Headquarters
11:18 AM GMT +3, 12Oct2000: *USS Cole* attacked by small boat carrying explosives during refueling stop in Aden, Yemen. Multiple US casualties and wounded. Ship seriously damaged. Suspected suicide terrorists. Evidence suggests Islamic militants.

Collins gave him a second to look over the bulletin, then asked, "So, Red, what are your thoughts?"

Red set his coffee cup down. Instead of addressing the telegram contents he frowned and said, "Y'know, Time Magazine ran a piece on *Piper Alpha*."

Though he didn't see any bearing on the current situation, the Lieutenant suspected it was there. He was learning that Red was sometimes indirect. "Oh yeah? They get their facts straight?"

"More than they know. The title was 'Disaster, Screaming Like a Banshee'."

"Sounds like there's more to that story than I've heard." Collins studied a matted photo on Red's wall. On one side of it was a framed purple heart, and beneath that was a black and white photo of some WWII Marines in front of what appeared to be a slain dragon.

"*Piper Alpha*'s what got me recruited." Red stared again at the report the man had handed him. "Yemen, the *USS Cole*." He rubbed his temples. "It's the damn *Stark* all over again."

"Hopefully not as many sailors this time," the Lieutenant said. He was on the other side of the matted photo, looking at a section of black cotton stretched over a square frame, a JTF13 patch stitched right into the center.

Red sighed and ran a hand through his thinning red hair. "Thirty-seven or three, we should be at war right now." He sat down, slumped forward, and put a palm to his forehead. "Dammit, Rick, I've gathered Intel on that demon for nearly ten years, but every time he slips through our fingers. Or we end up playing second fiddle to the conventional side, who go after the puppets rather than the one truly orchestrating this shit. Saxüru is behind ninety percent of what goes down over there, but I can't get support from my own chain of command, much less the pricks in charge of the purse strings. It's damn frustrating." He lifted his gaze to Rick. "We should be at war right now."

Rick furrowed his brow. "When have we not been at war? I mean, it's never official, but the conflict just never seems to end. And your chain of command does support you, at least the links in this division do."

Red nodded. "Points taken. Even so, someone needs to be held accountable. Those sailors deserve justice." Red never raised his voice, but his anger was palpable. "So, what's the mission?"

"We've seen indications that other-worldly creatures are being... disturbed. They want your expertise on the front lines. We're sending more forces into the region, upping our presence in the Gulf."

"I helped kill a Dendan when we bombed Baghdad in '91. You know, back when we failed to take out Saddam. If I'm going in, I'd like to know our conventional forces are gonna actually be allowed to finish their job this time."

"So would I." Lieutenant Collins shrugged. "Really wish I could give you a guarantee on that, but I can't."

"I know. Just venting."

"Listen, Chief, I understand your frustration completely. But until we get a definitive on who's responsible, I doubt you'll see a formal declaration. And with elections coming up, who knows..."

"So, when do I leave and where do I report?"

"You leave within the week. First stop is Camp Lemonnier."

Red gave a tired smile. "Great. Can't wait to break the news to Cassie. She's got her hands full, you know."

Rick smiled. "From what I could tell, you both do." He'd taken his own daughter to Abigail's fifth birthday a week prior. The chief's little girl was a small version of her mom, curious about everything with a never-ending stream of questions.

Red shook his head, still smiling. "That Abby will talk your ear off. And Hank may not say as much, but I swear it's a constant struggle just to keep him from accidentally killing himself or destroying everything we own." Red looked back up at Rick. "I'm assuming I'll be shipboard. If they really do want me on the front."

"Yep." Rick pushed his glasses snug against his face. "You're not gonna believe this, but here's what they have in mind..."

Chapter 34

October 15, 2000
Camp Lemonnier, Djibouti
1400 hours

Red stepped off the plane and looked around. Camp Lemonnier had changed, but only in regard to new metal buildings used as barracks and workspaces for the Marines leasing the area. He removed his mirrored shades to squint at a rangy figure shambling over in a rush.

Red broke into a smile. "Slim! Still hanging in there, I see."

"Good to see you too." The Texan put out a hand. "You old salt."

Red shook it. "When they said I was boarding the *Scorpius* I couldn't believe it. How's a tin can like her even seaworthy?"

Slim sniffed in mock disdain. "Had a helluva maintenance crew is how." He jerked a thumb toward a metal shed. "C'mon. Let's acquaint you with the others and then check on our lucky number seven. Got her upgraded with new engines, a bonafide state-of-the-art sonar system, all new weaponry, and—best of all—actual berthing racks with real two-inch foam mattresses."

As he followed Slim inside, Red was surprised to find even more familiar faces; Johnson, Shiv, Belfry, Dunc, Waymore, Doc, Smitty, and one he hadn't seen since Panama.

The marine had earned a few more stripes, along with a few more lines on his face, but was otherwise much the same. "Heard they got Facumama's mama up in this drainage ditch." Duffy raised a brow and gave a devilish grin. "Save a piece for me this time, whydoncha."

Red grinned and put a hand on the man's shoulder. "You got it, Duff." He turned to the ones he didn't recognize, all younger than his friends. "So, is this the Bravo team, or have I got things backwards?"

Shiv spoke up, "*Scorpius* finally has herself a full complement. We'll still be running with three shifts, but each will be integrated with veterans and newbies." She motioned to the new crewmen. Red shook hands as she spoke their names, "Derkins, Petroski, Baker, Elias, Carroll, Pelletier, and Garner." She glanced over as the door began to open. "And if I'm not mistaken, here's our fearless leader, which brings our roster to seventeen."

The figure was silhouetted by the bright afternoon sun pouring in around him. As the man stepped inside and shut the door, Red couldn't believe his eyes. "Morrison?"

The man wore civvies, had grayed considerably, but he was unmistakable as he smiled. "Red." He looked around the room. "All right, crew, let's go see our fine Lady."

"Hold on." Red put a hand to Morrison's elbow. "I thought you were retiring. Figured you'd be up in Maine by now, eating lobster with Helen's dad."

Belfry tried to stifle a laugh.

Morrison gave Belfry a sideways look then answered Red, "I got bored, okay. Besides, they made me an offer I couldn't refuse." He pulled something from his pocket and cupped it so only Red could see.

The metallic rank insignia of a silver oak leaf.

Red's eyes widened. "About time." Then he whispered, "So what's a full commander doing here?"

"Whatever he damn well pleases," said Morrison, aloud. "Besides…" He glanced around at the others. "Told 'em if I was coming back then they'd give me my rank, the command of my choice, and a hand-picked crew."

"So, you asked for us?" Johnson said, dumbfounded.

Morrison shrugged. "Well… I figured two out of three ain't bad."

"Somebody should write a song," said Waymore.

"I still got my ukulele," said Belfry. "Let's give 'er a go."

Red just shook his head. Time may have passed, but in that moment, he was awash in a flood of memories, most of them good. Before any bad ones could take roost, he opened the door and gestured for his captain to pass. "After you, sir."

Morrison stepped back outside and led them all toward the pier.

Chapter 35

October 17, 2000
The Red Sea, on the shore of Eritrea
Sunrise

Saxüru, still in the form of a Bedouin wanderer, gripped his staff and stood at the water's edge. He closed his eyes for a moment, taking in the sound of waves slapping hard against the land, the salty taste of windswept spray, but best of all the scent of decay from the carcasses littered about his feet.

Saxüru opened his eyes again and gave a sly smile. These earth-bound creatures had, in thirst crazed frenzies, stumbled, dashed, or staggered toward this false promise of drink, only to die on the brine-soaked shore. It was a deliciously grim parallel to the game of bait and switch he now played with the humans.

Things were falling into place. It was almost time.

The latest attack had caused several casualties and enough disturbance to free his largest beast. Called by various names — Falak, Leviathan, Orm — often to the point of confusion as to which civilization encountered it first, Saxüru simply preferred to think of it as his favorite pet.

He stepped into the choppy waters, wading out until knee deep, then lifted his staff horizontally and began the incantation. Calling to the creature, he bound it once again to his will. Then he ceased his chatter as the chilling north winds quieted. The Red Sea fell into eerie stillness.

Saxüru slowed his breathing, every sense attuned while he waited for a response. Finally, it came. Almost at once the sky darkened as roiling clouds tumbled southward. Raging winds whipped the waters into a tempest of chaotic waterspouts that ran in jagged, unpredictable lines. Lightning ripped the air and thunder cracked the sky.

He grinned, exposing yellowed canines, long and pointed as fangs. His serpent was now fully awakened and eager to do its master's bidding.

"Good. Good. Now let the Red Sea earn her name."

Deep within the trenches, the great serpent slumbered. Sated by an early morning meal of human flesh, it rested inside a cold, meandering stretch of silt. And then, instantly, it snapped awake, sensing that for which it waited. A familiar call, the summoning.

Sound rippled through the water in a steady, chattering stream. Ancient, enchanting, it came as a remembered vibration. Enthralling.

Yes, the serpent answered back. Then more vigorously, violently, as it found courage in the call. At once everything flooded into the forefront of its mind, and the great serpent knew its place. Recognizing the voice, it raced to answer that call.

I hear you, master. I will come and kill them all!

Chapter 36

October 21, 2000
The Red Sea
1400 hours

Chief Boatswain's Mate Ortiz stood on the weather deck yelling at one of his latest recruits to 'heave about on that line!' They were about to take on fuel in the middle of the Red Sea, and it took everyone pulling to get the nozzle and hose suspended between the two ships. Once the huge brass nozzle passed the halfway point it would pick up speed and, if they'd done their job right, slip right up to the diesel port and snug right on with one last pull. Ortiz smiled as his men got in sync with one another and heaved as one, chanting an old refrain: "Oh-we-oh-yo-oh!"

He chided them. "What's that? Some pirate crap you got from a movie?"

"A Metallica song, Chief," one of them yelled back.

"At least you boys got good taste in music." Ortiz laughed. "Now get that nozzle in and let's top her off!"

He was watching the nozzle sail through the air when he spotted something between their ship and the horizon. A flash of movement in the water. A chill ran down his spine. He discretely fetched a set of binoculars from a mounted toolbox. Scanning with the naked eye, he spotted it again and raised the binocs to his face.

He found it. Scaled, moving just below the surface, but winking in out of the waves, were fins the color of blood. It took him back to the time he spotted a mer-devil off the coast of Scotland, after he'd relieved his buddy McCraith as they answered the May-day call from *Piper Alpha*.

He'd had the good sense then to keep his mouth shut. Unlike Red, who disappeared soon after they reached port, when the ship was crawling with naval intelligence or whoever those spooks were, with all their questions and secrecy.

Damn, that was so long ago.

Ortiz tracked with the creature, trying not to call attention to himself or whatever it was in the sea. Then he saw it heave up momentarily, as if changing direction. A red-scaled bulge of serpentine flesh rose from the water and followed after itself in a spiraling wheel that sank back down until it disappeared.

The chief put the binoculars away. None of his men seemed to have noticed it. The beast, whatever it was, was massive. Should he say something? He was so close to retirement now, just a few more years.

No, he decided. He'd let it be. Whatever he'd seen was on its way down, probably never to be seen again. He looked again at his men. So strong. Young, mostly stubborn, but good kids. With any luck, nothing would ever come of this and he'd take it to his grave, along with the mer-thing he'd seen back when he was their age.

He genuflected and touched the crucifix tucked on a chain beneath his uniform. "Lord Jesus, in Your Holy Name, I bind all evil spirits of the air, water, and netherworld, any and all emissaries of the satanic realm and claim the Precious Blood. Heavenly Father, allow Your Son Jesus to come now with the Holy Spirit, the Blessed Virgin Mary, the holy angels and the saints to protect my men from all harm and to keep all evil spirits from plotting against us upon this ancient Sea."

Ortiz opened his eyes, looked skyward then back out across the water. As the diesel began to flow through the hose and into his ship, he whispered, "Amen."

They'd inspected the ship fore and aft and everything in-between. Within a few days it was fueled up, ready for its first run. Everyone came aboard. They would steam for five days then return to Lemonnier, a chance for everyone to rotate through their shifts and positions, conduct various drills and exercises, then debrief back at the camp and let the chain of command know they were battle ready and standing by for further instruction.

As Morrison took command and ordered the helm to take her to sea, he got a strange feeling in his gut. A feeling he'd learned to trust, even if he couldn't explain it. He looked around at his crew. "I know this is a test run," he said, "But things can turn on a dime. If we got called into battle today, I want all of you to know we can handle it. We're stocked up on rations, got plenty of water, armory is fully loaded and all weapons ready if we need them."

"And one helluva crew, sir." Red gave a one-sided smile, a glint in his eye.

And just like that Morrison knew he wasn't the only one. *You feel it too, you sly bastard.* Heck, probably all of the old-timers did. He put his hand on a section of metal hull inside the bridge. How could anyone not feel it? The sea, the *Scorpius*, even the air they breathed seemed to vibrate with foreboding.

He took a last glance around at them. Not a one seemed afraid. On alert, sure. Like cats ready to pounce, or a steel trap with a hair trigger. In spite of himself, Morrison grinned. "All righty then. Let's get her up on the foils and go raise some hell."

Chapter 37

October 21, 2000
The Red Sea
1440 hours

The ship completed refueling and sent hoses and lines back across to the German oiler. The entire time Ortiz never left the deck. Though unsure exactly what he'd seen, he knew it was otherworldly, had felt it as a chill in his bones. He determined to stay with his detail until he was certain the men were all safe and the threat, which only he seemed to notice, had passed.

Their vessel pulled away from the oiler, then began a slow turn to starboard so the ship they steamed with could pull alongside to repeat the process. An announcement came over the 1MC, "Underway replenishment is now complete. All hands prepare for maneuvers to take lifeguard station."

As the refueling detail stashed all their gear and began to disperse, Ortiz sent up a silent prayer of thanks. Most of the men would lay below to eat a late lunch, others would have a lunch put aside for later, while they took on their next duty: to help ensure the safety of the other crew.

The ship soon fell into place a few thousand yards astern of the oiler and its next customer. The U.S. naval ships had basically swapped positions. All so they could take turns, watching in case a deckhand fell overboard while heaving lines across.

Ortiz took the binoculars again and found the man he was searching for. A young sailor, standing near the rail of the oiler. He lifted a pneumatic gun to his shoulder and took aim. The cylindrical weighted bag shot through the air, dragging its light 'messenger line' across the distance.

It landed on the deck of the naval ship. A boatswain's mate hurried over and retrieved it, which soon led to the initial pull which ferried the relay lines into place. Within minutes the crew of the other ship were heaving on the line to pull the nozzle and hose across the suspension rigging.

Ortiz studied the men in their large life vests, glowing chemical lights tied and hanging from the front of each man's chest. Though sunlight was fading, they should finish refueling before sunset. Still, if a storm came out of nowhere, as it sometimes did, the lights would help find a man in the darkness.

He shuddered. Even as he thought these things the glow sticks seemed to brighten. He eased the binocs from his eyes and turned his head. Over his left shoulder he spotted the cloud. Great. Here was the storm right on cue. Thunderheads rolled into his peripheral vision.

He wasn't the only one to notice. One of his men pointed toward the storm.

"Eyes on your job, sailor!" Ortiz shouted across to him. "I'll call the quarterdeck."

He moved to a nearby phone box and opened it, picked up the handset and turned the selector switch to the circuit. He let the officer of the deck know in case the lookouts hadn't yet. He was informed the two ships ahead were aware and would be cutting the refueling short. The captain on the receiving end wanted to top off, but would settle for 95% of his capacity, which would cut their time in half.

"Roger that, sir," Ortiz said to the lieutenant on the other end. He put the handset in its cradle and shut the metal door. "Their old man should have his ass out on that deck," he mumbled.

It was a never-ending string of unnecessary decisions that he realized long ago he'd never understand. He knew they had to stay battle ready, but these COs who insisted on staying topped off, never letting their ship go below 85%. Sometimes it made sense, but other times it absolutely didn't.

Like now, for instance, with the wind picking up and the waves beginning to roll. Even crawling along at 12 knots, with the ships so close that a course drift of one degree could end up in a collision. Men could go overboard or even get killed.

He furrowed his brow at the scene ahead. The captain of that oiler had probably given the old man a firm no and called the refueling to a halt. As the delivering ship, the final call was his. "Good on him." Ortiz grinned.

The ships were already beginning breakaway. At least somebody cared about the men on the deck, the guys without all the plush wardrooms and scrambled eggs on the brims of their caps.

Then he realized this was no normal breakaway. He noticed what the other crews had obviously already seen: a serpentine movement on the waves beyond them. "Mary, Mother of God," he whispered. He watched as the vessels performed an emergency breakaway. Nozzles disengaged and hoses quickly ferried over, followed by lines which were untied and sent back to the oiler as the ships began to move apart.

"Clear the weather decks!" Ortiz yelled to his men, even as his own ship began evasive maneuvers. He needed to get them below decks, away from whatever that thing was. At least until someone could figure things out. To their credit, the crew obeyed without hesitation.

Ortiz was the last one on deck and had yet to step through the open door, watching in horror as something like an immense serpent, the color of fresh blood, lifted its wide, scaled head far above the surface — high as the bridge windows. His insides turned to jelly.

"You coming, Chief?" It was Milford, one of his first-class petty officers, calling from inside.

The chief nodded, but kept a grip on the handle, transfixed by the monstrous beast. He rasped. "Get below. And get ready for… I don't even know. Maybe Hell itself." He didn't look at Milford, just listened as the man's footsteps faded away.

The creature shrieked. Huge, scalloped ears, almost like wings, flared from either side of its skull. Water shivered into the air as the winding column of flesh trembled in fury. Two long tusks hung from its lower jaw. Its mouth was a mass of daggered teeth. A line of fins ran down its spine. Three short, sharp horns jutted in a row, spear-like, starting between its scaled brow with the last one just above the base of its skull.

Chief Ortiz gasped as the creature lashed out at the men still on deck of the oiler. It snatched one into its mouth, impaling another with a curved tusk. Then the thunderclouds overtook everything, casting all into shadow as rain began to fall.

The 1MC blared to life, relaying orders through speakers mounted on every deck, "General Quarters, General Quarters, all hands man your battle stations…" Finally, Ortiz stepped inside and dogged the door behind him. He let out a deep breath. "God help us all."

Chapter 38

October 21, 2000
The Red Sea
1445 hours

The *Scorpius* had just completed her sortie. She was headed to anchor in a nearby bay when a call came through: "Mayday mayday, we are under attack. Priority Metal, Red Silver! Repeat, mayday, under attack. Priority…"

The distress call was over open airwaves, but the JTF fire call protocol clearly marked it as U.S. Navy. Everyone on the bridge got to work. "Check secure comms. See if anything else is coming through," said Morrison. Without waiting he got on the radio. "This is November Whiskey Sierra Lima, copy your distress call. Determining your position and our ETA."

He paused while, down in CIC, Red and Shiv opened the lock box to pull out a cipher sheet. There were encrypted coordinates coming through. They did a quick authentication with the distressed vessel and, with mutual trust established, deciphered the info. Red soon gave Morrison the ship's name and position while Shiv continued comms over the secure channel.

She scuttled to her charts and started plotting. "Sir, we're fifteen minutes out, top speed. Bearing three four seven."

"Roger that," Morrison said, "Helm, put us there. Full speed."

"Yes sir." Duncan was already getting them up on the foils.

Captain Morrison picked up the mic for the 1MC. "General Quarters. All hands to battle stations. Gunners, ready weapons. In fifteen minutes, we'll engage a creepy-crawly. Conventional forces are under attack and we're the only Team Spooky in town. Let's rain down death, people."

The hatch to the bridge opened and Red stepped through. He had an M16 and a belt of ammo. "Any idea yet what we're up against?"

Shiv looked up, a worried expression on her face. "Some kinda sea serpent." She pressed a hand against her earpiece. "They estimate it at two hundred feet long. Five casualties so far."

Morrison noted her trepidation. "Chin up, people. They may be better armed than we are. But they have no grid for this. We do."

"Enter Caelum..." Red began, which coaxed a smile from Shiv.

"...Et Infernum," she finished.

The captain watched from the bridge with disbelief as the thing wrapped itself around the German oiler. The immense creature was raking across the deck with its tusks, mouth agape. The men aboard the ship were shooting with rifles and handguns to no avail. The bullets seemed to spark against its scales, ricocheting away. With ease it killed another three men.

Having sent out the distress call and gotten a reply from the *Scorpius*, the man was not content to simply wait. "I'm open to options," he announced to the others.

His officer of the deck replied, "Sir, we can't fire our five-inch guns. Can't blast it with an ASROC or Harpoon. Too risky with the oiler there."

The captain frowned. "Don't tell me what I can't do, Lieutenant. I said I wanted options."

"Captain Newman," said the boatswain's mate steering the ship. "What about the sea wiz?"

He was referring to the Phalanx CIWS, *Close in Weapons System*. Normally reserved for airborne threats, it could fire armor piercing 20 x 120mm rounds into anti-ship missiles and helos at a rate of 3000 rounds per minute.

Commander Newman replied, "Not bad, but our R2 unit has more than a few limitations." The weapon resembled the famous droid in shape if not function, and so was often called that. "It fires using radar input," the captain informed him. "If the target moves too slow, it won't engage. If it's not approaching or edging closer, it won't engage. More for missiles than sea monsters. But I like the way you're thinking. Anyone else?"

"Get us closer," offered the quartermaster. "Put some of our men on the deck with weapons from the armory. Maybe hit it with five inch if we get a clean shot."

Newman squinted and gave a slow nod. "Let's move in, but not too close. And get someone on a .50 cal. We can also use a few men with M16s. But we won't be using our five-inch. Like the lieutenant said, we don't want to accidentally hit a ship full of fuel. I want a headshot. Aim for the eyes. Those can't be armored. With any luck, whatever brain this thing has is nested behind the eye socket."

"Sir," the lieutenant interjected, "With that thing so close to the oiler, I don't know if we should even..."

Newman waved him to silence and sighed. "I know, but in the meantime, men are dying, and we can't afford to do nothing. We'll target the head. Hit it with as much firepower as we can. With any luck, when the cavalry arrives, they can help pick up the carcass."

The officer of the deck furrowed his brow. "What cavalry? That call sign corresponds to a Pegasus Class hydrofoil." He picked up the phone to contact the master at arms and get the plan in action. He mumbled as he waited for the man to pick-up, "Didn't even know we had one over here."

Newman kept his eyes on the creature. "Ask me again when this is over. Maybe I'll even tell you. Helm, bring us five degrees to port."

Twelve minutes later

The *Scorpius* cut through the storm at full speed. Red looked around at his crewmates. Unless directly involved in driving the *Scorpius* or running vital equipment, everyone had automatic rifles, side arms, even knives strapped to their thighs. They also wore body armor and helmets. He turned his attention to the scene rapidly approaching.

Thick clouds, dark and menacing sent down a wall of water, even as wind churned the sea into a roiling frenzy. Froth splatted upon the windows as rain obscured everything beyond.

Then thunder cracked as lightning struck nearby. An explosion followed on its heels as the oiler ignited, sending up a fireball that backlit three ships in stark relief.

In the sudden illumination, Red, along with everyone on the bridge, saw everything.

The oiler had a burst hull, spilling fuel and taking on water. The Navy vessels pitched and rolled on twenty-foot waves. One of them, a U.S. vessel, had men outside, harnessed to masts or rails in what they must know was a desperate suicide mission. Each man fired as he had opportunity.

And right in the midst of it all was the beast.

Its tail wound tight to the nose of the oiler. The majority of its body dropped into the depths, effectively concealing its length. The head shook maniacally upon a scaled, curved pedestal of a neck.

The creature had apparently breached the hull with its death grip. Leaking fuel burned on the churning sea around the crippled oiler.

In a moment, the torrential downpour slackened to sheets of intermittent rain. Red studied the beast, looking for a vulnerable spot. It was then he noticed its tusks, one which skewered a dead man who was dressed as part of the oiler crew. Atop its spiked head a uniformed sailor, impaled through the torso flailed weakly.

The unmistakable blasts of a .50 cal roared to life. Sparks danced up the serpent's throat. As it dodged aside, one tore through an ear, punching a hole through the membrane and sent a splatter of blood around the hole. The creature gave a screech that rattled the windows.

Red noted the foreign naval ship, tracking well away from the wreckage, while the U.S. ship was slowly distancing itself, whether retreat or a tactical maneuver, it was unclear.

"Oh hell," Slim mumbled.

Red clenched his jaw and gripped his weapon with grim determination. "We're trained for this. Let's do our thing."

Morrison picked up the mic. "*USS John Wayne*, this is the *Scorpius*, advise on your maneuvers."

The airwaves crackled. "...Thing is damn near indestructible. We're gonna back off and hit it with a harpoon."

"What about the oiler?" Morrison scanned with a set of binoculars.

"She's lost. Steer clear so you don't get caught in the blast."

"Captain, stand down! There are men in the water. I'm sure their damage control team is actively securing compartments. Let the *Scorpius* handle it."

There was a pause, followed by a click, an audible sigh, and then, "Okay, *Scorpius*, I'll give you a window, but finish this quick, or I will give the order to fire."

Morrison flew hot. "That wasn't a suggestion! Nor was it a request for permission. As the ranking 13 officer I'm now taking command of a situation *you* are not trained to deal with. All orders are to come through me."

"*Scorpius*, be advised. I've already lost men. You have a window. Use it. If you don't kill that damn thing soon, we will launch anything we can against it."

"Commander Newman," Morrison said, to make it clear that he knew the man's name, "Any order to that effect and I'll see you court martialed."

"...son of a bitch. I'll see *you* court martialed—again! I'm only gonna—"

Morrison turned down the squawk box. "I don't have time for this!" He kept his eyes forward. "Let's get in there, hit it with our big guns. Aim for the head and shred it to bits. Don't care if we gather any evidence."

He got back on the mic. "Hold your fire. Your five inch is too big, and harpoons are off the table. We'll hit it with our front mount. Stay clear until we kill this thing and standby to pull survivors from the sea."

With the *Scorpius* hull borne again, they approached the creature straight on. The weapons team set the forward mount and prepared to fire.

Red felt a sudden drop in temperature. "Y'all feel that?" he asked.

"Something supernatural," said Dunc.

"Duh, the snake," said Duffy.

They were almost within range.

Red shook his head. "It's not the snake."

Morrison held up a fist for everyone to quiet down and the gun crew to standby to fire. The instant they were in range he gave the command, "Fire."

The forward gun spit out a hail of ammo. The creature jerked its head, surprised as rounds tattooed across its hide, ripping through its other ear and tearing into flesh in at least three places.

Before the spray of bullets could reach its eyes the monster dove. Morrison watched as the tail slipped free of the oiler. "Water's too rough to run on foils. Commence evasive maneuvers, pull away but watch for men in the water."

As the *Scorpius* began to zigzag through the waves, Red warned them all, "That thing isn't stupid. We've just tipped our hand with the big gun, so I doubt it's gonna give us or that destroyer a clear shot."

Morrison nodded. "I'm guessing it'll stay close to the oiler. It's not just killing those men. It's eating them." He kept his eyes forward but spoke to the crew. "But it does bleed, which means it can die. For now, we fall back and regroup."

He picked up the mic, "*John Wayne* this is the *Scorpius*. Status of your ASROCs?"

"Change your mind on collateral damage?"

"Hell no. Do you have sonar on that snake and are your ASROCs ready or not?"

"Affirmative on both," came the terse reply. "That thing's curled up under the oiler. Keeping out of sight now and doesn't look like it's budging. So, what's the plan?"

"This line isn't secure. I'll tell you as you need to know."

"Do you actually believe that beast can hear and understand us? Of all the stupid…"

Morrison turned down the volume again, as the captain continued to rant.

Red got up close so no one else could hear. "You saw him, too, didn't you?"

Morrison gave an almost imperceptible nod. "Saxüru's hanging onto a fin about halfway down the serpent's back."

"I'm thinking we need to get Saxüru off that perch," Red whispered, "Separate the brains from the brawn."

"Any ideas?"

Red grinned. "Yeah, but you're probably not gonna like it."

Chapter 39

October 21, 2000
The Red Sea
1500 hours

Upon the ragged back of his undulating serpent, Saxüru chattered softly, reassuring the beast. "Feast on the fallen, my pet. See how they slowly sink and are forced deeper by my waves. I brought this storm upon the humans. Now I bring this flesh down for you. Is it not delectable, the taste of their flesh, the sweetness of their fear, the agony of their deaths?"

The snake jerked forward, snatching a drowning man in its jaws. It thrust its head forward and back, forcing the man further down its throat, swallowing in vicious increments.

Saxüru's senses ignited in a single heartbeat. That scent! It was more than just human blood. It was the blood of a particular human; one he had learned to despise.

"I remember you!" he chattered aloud. To the serpent he said, "Wait here, Falak. Your master must attend to an enemy. This is the one who lured my queen in the North water to her death. I swore vengeance on that day. Attempted to send a swarm of my sharks to shred him to bits, but they were too late. This time, I shall do the deed myself. Stay beneath the waves, this will not take long."

On the deck of the *Scorpius*, Red wiped the bloodied knife on his breeches and sheathed it. He closed his sliced palm into a fist and squeezed, sending a few more drops of blood into the sea. "That should do it."

"What makes you think this'll do any good at all? That's what I want to know," said Morrison.

"Our Intel. All the stuff we learned from Gurax. Saxüru will take this bait."

"Here he comes!" shouted Belfry from down in CIC, manning the sonar.

Morrison keyed the squawk box, "*USS John Wayne*, you should see a contact break away from the serpent."

A pause, then static, and "Affirmative, moving really fast in your direction."

"Can you intercept with an ASROC?" He referred to the anti-submarine rockets mounted on the destroyer's fantail.

"It's risky, but with any luck we should be able to catch it halfway between you and the oiler."

"Do it. One ASROC, make it count."

"Sending over the side now."

Morrison brought a set of binocs to his eyes, found the destroyer, and watched as the MK-112, or matchbox as most called the launch assembly, swung around to port and sent a single missile over the side and into the water.

Saxüru shot through the currents, one thing on his mind. The scent of blood. Which had to mean the man was overboard and wounded. Easy prey. Saxüru grinned as he lunged forward, fast as he could swim. If wounded, he would finish the man. If dead already, that would be unfortunate, but either way he would feast on human flesh. Even better, the flesh of a despised enemy.

Along the lateral scales of his left side, Saxüru felt a strange vibration, signaling a streak of movement through the water. He chanced the slightest glance in that direction, caught sight of the weapon. Closing distance with him, it moved at an alarming rate. He tried to evade but the weapon slammed into his torso. An explosion rocked the sea, cracking his bones in a deafening blast.

Saxüru slumped, helpless, as everything went black.

Chapter 40

October 21, 2000
The Red Sea
1505 hours

Red and Dunc were on either side of the *Scorpius*, M16s at the ready. The three-inch gun was set to fire, though it would probably be useless at close range. Red was really hoping for the ASROC to do its job. Praying Saxüru would be so incensed by the smell of his blood, that the goat-fish would drop his guard and not notice the missile closing in until it was too late.

A sudden shockwave rocked the Seas. "Direct hit!" Belfry screamed up from the lower deck.

Red held off on celebrating. The surface bulged as the underwater blast swelled the water in a huge irregular circle. A limp body floated up with it. He yelled over to Dunc, "Make sure that thing is dead!"

They positioned themselves and opened fire on the floating body. Bullets tore into the demi-god's flesh, riddling it with holes.

"Get off that deck!" Morrison yelled. "We're gonna tear it a new one."

Red and Dunc slipped inside the bridge. "Go for it," said Dunc.

Morrison gave the order. The forward mount shifted, its three-inch barrel locking in on the position. A single round punched a hole in the center of the goat-thing's back, ripping its torso from its huge fish-like tail.

Red watched as the serpent broke the surface. It writhed, shrieking, and churning the water, using its barbed tail as a whip. The creature thrashed, sending water skyward in thick arcing sheets that splashed and swirled all around, effectively obscuring everything. Red caught movement in his periphery and turned just in time to see the tail lash out across the fantail, striking the Harpoon launchers.

The two quad RGM-84 Harpoon assemblies broke away from the deck and were pulled toward the starboard rail by a writhing mass of muscle, bone, and scale. The *Scorpius* lurched to one side, dragged askew as the launcher caught momentarily, only to rip through the railing and plop loudly into the sea.

"Hold on!" Red yelled, as he grabbed a cable with one hand. He saw Dunc do the same. The starboard deck slipped beneath the waves for just a moment, then sent water sloughing across to the port side as the ship righted itself while the serpent's tail slipped away.

Lightning bolts ripped through the sky with loud thunderclaps as a scaled hide emerged, rising like a scarlet spire against the darkness. Right in front the *Scorpius*.

The beast jerked and shrieked in pain. A volley of bullets ripped into its hide about halfway up the neck.

On the deck, both Dunc and Red had crouched behind the superstructure, shielding themselves from the sound of the 76 mm. But Red couldn't resist. Neither could Dunc. In a coordinated move, they both stood and leveled weapons at the monster's head. A spray of lead from their M16s kicked across the hard scales of the serpent's face, ricocheting off hide and teeth.

Both men had aimed for the eyes, but the beast wouldn't sit still, and neither would the ship. The storm was rising again, pitching the ship on waves of ever-increasing size. The wounded serpent shoved its head to one side and then dove beneath the waves.

Chapter 41

October 21, 2000
The Red Sea
1510 hours

Saxüru felt a tendril of consciousness pull him from the brink of death's abyss. A tenuous link still tied him to the living creature, interrupting his passage into hell. With that one thread connecting him to life, Saxüru dragged himself toward the creature and then latched on.

The serpent calmed at first, reassured by the return of its master, then felt a dread chill as Saxüru's consciousness asserted itself fully into the seat of the monster's soul. At that, the snake rebelled, unwilling to yield full control, instinctively knowing what such a submission would mean.

It pushed back in desperation. Resisted the betrayal with all its might. But in the end, it was no use, Saxüru was too strong.

With the strength of his will, Saxüru took complete possession. Subduing the body, then quickly severing ties with the soul of the great beast. In a final merciless shove, Saxüru sent his pet to hell in his stead.

Though he could not chatter with the serpent's mouth as he had with his own, the demi-god flexed in glorious triumph. Fully in control, he finally noticed the wounds marring the creature's flesh. He assessed the damage, careful to keep himself beneath the waves.

Though bleeding, he sensed the wounds were superficial. He would not die. Saxüru shrieked in renewed confidence. Now he would make the humans pay.

Once the three-inch guns stopped, Morrison opened the bridge door and stuck his head out. "Red, Dunc, get your asses in here!"

As they stepped in from opposite sides and dogged the doors behind, Shiv said, "So did we kill it?"

"No," Red answered. "But we wounded it. No doubt about that."

"Which makes it dangerous," said Morrison. "Let's get some distance between us and that thing."

But before the order could be carried out, the creature erupted again from the brine. This time it arced above the three-inch, looping itself across the gun's barrel. A second loop wrapped over its first, falling in front of the bridge, obstructing the view. A third loop slid behind the superstructure. The beast coiled its head and open wounds safely beneath the waves. It began to squeeze.

"We're taking on water!" Belfry exclaimed. "Waymore and some others are running damage control. But if we don't kill that thing quick—"

"It's gonna take us under," Morrison finished.

Red growled, "We just need to get it to surface and cut off the damn head. Everyone on deck with M16s, sending streams of lead across its neck, point blank."

Morrison sighed. "Wish it was that easy. No way is it coming back up. It's gonna sink the *Scorpius*."

"So, what do we do?" asked Dunc.

"Abandon ship," said Morrison.

"Like hell," Red protested.

Morrison shook his head. "It's not a request. It's an order." He picked up the 1MC. "All hands abandon ship. Get to the weather decks and put on a life vest. Swim as far away from the *Scorpius* and the *USS John Wayne* as possible."

When he put down the mic, Red asked, "Sir, what are you doing?"

In response he got on the squawk box. "*USS John Wayne*, this is the *Scorpius*. We are abandoning ship. Give us ten minutes and then harpoon the hell out of this beast."

A moment of static and then, "*USS Scorpius*, understand. We'll give you as much time as we can, and we will end that monster."

"Ten minutes," Morrison repeated. "I want my people clear of the blast."

"Okay. Ten minutes. And once we kill that thing, I'm putting priority on pulling your men from the water."

"No," said Morrison. "Get the survivors from that oiler. My crew will stay together. Swim to a single position so you can find us. We'll send up a flare when we're ready or if things get dicey."

"Roger that." A pause. "Godspeed, Morrison."

"*Scorpius* out."

As the crew moved to carry out the orders, Red moved close enough to whisper. "When we go in the water, what's to keep that thing from eating us? Have you even thought of that?"

Morrison gave a solemn stare. "That's why I'm going in first." He swallowed hard. "Give me thirty seconds, then get everyone to safety. And tell Helen that I love her." He shoved a flare gun into Red's hands.

"No. There's got to be some other way."

But the captain wasn't listening. By now everyone had put on life jackets and armed themselves with bang sticks and knives. Crewmembers were hurrying up from below decks and mustering on the fantail to await further orders. "Everyone do what Red tells you!" Morrison said, as he ripped the back off his captain's seat and grabbed something from inside.

With no explanation Morrison exited the bridge and did the unthinkable, running toward the nose of the *Scorpius*, wind and waves pounding him. He went over the side as a bolt of lightning illuminated him in a single frame, searing the image into Red's mind. Upside down, diving headfirst into the waves, clenching a thick, 18-inch iron barb in his fist.

Chapter 42

October 21, 2000
The Red Sea
1512 hours

Saxüru waited beneath the surface, taking a moment to strategize. Then a splash nearby caught his attention. A human. His first instinct was to rush in and devour the fool, but he thought better of it. Having underestimated the humans before, he realized it may simply be a distraction. Or a trap.

He noticed the barb held tightly in the man's fist. The man was a fool. Did he truly think he could assail the serpent single-handed with no more than that?

Saxüru's mind raced. He had seen such behavior before. Had instigated it in fact. This was an act of desperation, an intentional suicide mission.

Saxüru pulled back, keeping the man in sight, while continuing to drag the vessel under. Soon the others would be forced into the water, whether they were ready or not. Surely this one meant to delay him while the others made their escape.

But it would not work. The demi-god squeezed again, pulling downward. He felt the metal hull crack, knew it was taking on water. The man changed course, no longer swimming for his head. Giving up perhaps.

Then Saxüru noticed how close the human was to his own sinuous body. He watched as the puny thing grabbed the base of a dorsal fin.

Saxüru shook in a violent quake. Undulating, he sent a trembling ripple along the muscles beneath his skin. But still the man held on.

"Now!" Red shouted. "Everyone in. Follow me and stay close." He dove from the aft deck, even as water began flooding over it. The others all followed behind him. The last one with hardly any distance between the deck and the surface.

Red looked back once to make sure everyone was in the water. He watched as the *Scorpius* slipped beneath the waves, then turned and swam like hell.

"Dammit!" Belfry yelled. "That snake just pulled Johnson under!"

Red turned and headed in Belfry's direction. "Waymore, lead them outta here!"

"Hell with that!" came the reply.

Belfry struggled and swiped at the water with the blade in his hand. Blood pooled to the surface as he went under. Like Red, everyone converged on that spot, knives in hand.

Morrison stabbed at the serpent's eye with his iron barb. Though a hard, transparent shell covered the eyeball, the membrane was not as hard as the scales of the hide. With the first blow it cracked. With the second it gave way, and the iron shaft sank deep. Blood flooded the water, enveloping Morrison in a dark red cloud.

The serpent rose from the water. Rising high into the storm charged air, it shook its head in pain and fury. Morrison held fast to the thing's head. "Get outta here!" he raged above the storm. "That's an order!"

Red was treading water, along with the others. "You all heard him. Let's go."

"We've still got these." Waymore brandished a blade.

Red lost it, screaming in reply, "And they won't penetrate that hide! Don't make our captain lose any more of his crew."

Shiv started swimming. "He's right. We owe him that much."

Red followed after her, away from the thrashing beast which was still trying to dislodge Morrison. Though reluctant, the others all fell in alongside.

"We've waited long enough," the destroyer captain said to his men. "Launch Harpoons. Let's kill that thing."

Chapter 43

October 21, 2000
The Red Sea
1520 hours

With one hand on the blade and his other holding onto the creature's third horn, Morrison straddled the creature's head. It was like riding a steer back in Texas. Only he intended to hang on for much longer than eight seconds. Then from the corner of his eye, he saw the flash. "Dear God, please let them swim clear."

Spaced two seconds apart, the harpoons were launched in a volley that rocked the destroyer and lit up the sky. On the heels of the second missile came a third. The third missile streamed through the air, skimming above the sea at over 500 mph.

The 488-pound warhead met with the beast's armored hide and tore its head from the neck. The second missile tore through the snake's midsection, ripping it in half. In the final throes of death, coils of flesh thrashed about, slapping the water in random spasms. The third, final missile made impact near the surface where the *Scorpius* had gone under. It exploded, sending what remained of the creature in a dozen directions. The shockwave rent the air and ripped across the water.

Red and the others watched it all. Close enough to see their captain die, but far enough to survive the force of the three blasts. Still, their ears rang in the aftermath. Red's vision blurred, but not from any shockwave or flying debris.

Though surrounded by a briny sea, his vision was obscured by the small but steady stream of tears that he refused to keep in. He didn't sob, but he saw that others did. And he let them. No one said a word. Not that they could even hear each other yet, over the ringing in their ears. But they didn't need to. Tear filled glances confirmed the sorrow, the weight of loss that each of them felt.

Finally, Red huddled them together. Reaching out, they all formed a circle. Battered, bruised, and scarred in more ways than one. But they were alive.

The sea began to calm, and they noticed the clouds had rolled away. They waited while the destroyer closed distance and began to pick up survivors from the oiler. A boat was deployed from the ship's side and moved from place to place, pulling in the burned and bleeding then ferrying them away from the wreckage and onto the destroyer. Soon another convoy of ships arrived to help in the search and rescue.

After enough time had passed, Red took out the flare and sent up a signal. "Come get my people," he whispered into the wind. "Pull us out of this bloody mess and get us home."

"Get 'em up here, but be careful," Chief Ortiz firmly encouraged his men. "They might be wounded."

The boat had tied alongside, and its crew was helping the last load of survivors aboard.

Red insisted everyone else go up first. Then it was just him, Smitty, and the boat crew.

"Sir," said the young boatswain's mate, "I mean, I know you're not officers. Probably not anyway, but…" the young man was floundering, clearly out of sorts over the day's events.

"It's okay," Red told him. "I know. It's time to go." He looked to Smitty. "You first, bro. I'll be right behind."

Smitty nodded and got to his feet, following the younger man up the lattice of ropes on unsteady legs.

Red felt it too, as he fell in behind and clutched the coarse fibers of the wet, sagging grid. Bone tired is what he was. He looked up to see Smitty being helped over the rail, then started his own upward slog, one weary foot after the other.

It was almost over, he told himself. Soon he could rest again. Red alternated hands and feet, ever higher up the ropes. He was barely to the top when two strong BM3s grabbed him, one to each arm, and helped him aboard.

He ambled over next to Smitty. Looked at his friend and gave a weak smile. "This how you felt when we cut you outta that fish?"

Smitty winced. "Nah. That was twice as bad."

Red shrugged. "So, this is more like a cricket with a hook shoved halfway up his ass?"

His friend nodded. "That's about right."

Then Red heard a vaguely familiar voice.

"C'mon men, let's get 'em to sick bay," the chief boatswain's mate ordered his deck crew. "Let doc check them over and get 'em all settled."

Red steadied himself on the nearest stanchion. There were years and weight on the man, but it was him all right. "Ortiz?" he ventured.

The chief's eyes widened. He blinked and then squinted at each of them as recognition sank in.

"Sweet Virgin Mary..." His jaw dropped as he genuflected. He made an effort of composing himself then said, "Red? Smitty?"

"Damn, Ortiz," said Smitty, "You've put on some pounds."

Chief Ortiz smiled, made a show of flexing and bowing out his chest. "Moved to a higher weight class. Don't make me put you in the sleeper hold."

Red grinned. "Two at a time, right?"

Ortiz gently put a hand on each man's shoulder. Quietly he said, "Damn straight. Now let's get you guys down to the corpsman." He turned to his men. "I've got these guys. You boys help the others get that boat back in place."

John S. Worth

Chapter 44

October 21, 2000
The Red Sea, aboard the *USS John Wayne*
1900 hours

Ortiz stayed with them most of the day, making sure they had everything they needed. That evening they dined in the Chief's mess.

"Got Captain Newman's okay on this," Ortiz said, once they'd had their fill. He pulled a small flask from his jacket and set three shot glasses on the table. "This is the good stuff," he said, smiling at Red. He poured a drink for each of them.

Red gave it a swirl and lifted it to his nose. His eyes widened. "Scotch. I'm impressed."

Ortiz grinned. "Just 'cause you got that head of thinning red hair, don't mean you're the only one learned to appreciate this stuff. I've seen the world. Got me some culture."

Smitty smelled his and closed his eyes. "Chivas Regal," he said, "Twenty-five year."

"Huh?" said Ortiz. "How'd you…"

"Like you said, we're all cultured now," said Smitty. "I'm a man of many undisclosed talents."

Red started laughing. "Your captain checked on us while you were in the shower. Said he owed you one and hoped we like his whiskey."

Smitty chimed in, "Especially seeing as how it was Chivas Regal 25 and unopened, until he poured half in your flask."

Ortiz shook his head and mumbled, "Cultured my ass. We're still just a bunch of old Deck Dawgs." He smiled and lifted his glass. "A toast." He grew somber as they lifted their shots to his. "To the *Scorpius*," he said.

"To her crew," Smitty added. "Belfry, Johnson—"

"Hank and Morrison," Red finished.

Ortiz raised an eyebrow. "Not Morrison from our *Hayler* days?

Red swallowed a tear that told only in his voice. "Yeah ... that Morrison."

Chief Mateo Ortiz gave a single nod. "Then to him especially, and all the others we've lost along the way."

They clinked the glasses together then downed them as one. Set them smartly down with a thump.

"Guys," said Ortiz, as he refilled their glasses. "Have I got some stories for you. Stuff you wouldn't believe…"

Smitty gave a sly grin. "Do tell?"

Chapter 45

February 10, 2001
Quantico, Virginia
0630 hours

With the *Scorpius* lost to the sea, its remaining crew was disbanded. Still, the higher ups took note of their sacrifice. Though the details couldn't be made public, a private ceremony was planned, and arrangements made for all of them to attend.

But still, Red felt he had a duty left unfinished. He'd presented his evidence to everyone who would listen, but in the end, it came to nothing.

"I've warned them," he said to Cassie over coffee one morning. "It's imminent. Any day now. But they won't listen. They can't interpret the data like I do." He was scanning the morning paper, picking out world events that seemed to confirm his latest theories on the intel he'd been seeing.

She pursed her lips in thought, then said, "Maybe you're just wrong. Ever consider that?"

He smiled. "Honey, I pray every day that I'm wrong."

"Then why not ease up on this? Just a little?" said Cassie. "We lost three good men, but you killed that monster. Two in fact. You protected the fleet." She put her good hand on her husband's arm. "Sweetie, you did your job."

He sighed. "That thing had contacts all over the Middle East. Hussein in Iraq, Khamenei, in Iran, Bin Laden, ties with Hamas. The list goes on."

Cassie took off her prosthetic arm and flattened the fingers, pressing them close together. She held it out, putting it right up in his face, a gesture she called 'giving him the hand'.

He smiled sadly and shook his head at her sign for him to stop. "Okay, okay," he said. "So, I'll go to the ceremony, accept my award with the rest of the crew, and keep my mouth shut about how all of this is just the tip of the iceberg." He paused, raising an eyebrow. "...for now."

A few months passed. Life was good, from all outside appearances. The kids were growing up strong and healthy. Red and Cassie were doing better than they ever had. But there was a sadness inside him. A gnawing, growing turmoil that just would not pass.

Red had been to the chaplain, been to the mandatory sessions with a JTF13 therapist, but still there were nightmares and days when he just couldn't seem to go on. Finally, Cassie suggested, "Why don't you call your Dad? He's been through this kind of thing. Maybe he could help."

Red just shook his head. "He won't. Doesn't like to talk about his time in the Task Force, so I don't see how it would help to burden him with mine."

"Okay," she said. "Then let's just go for a visit. Get away for a week." She smiled. "Let your mama cook you some of her biscuits. The ones shaped like big cat-heads that you like to eat with cane syrup?"

He smiled at her attempt of his description. "They're just *big* as cat heads, darling. That's all. There's no ears or whiskers. But sure, I'll give them a call."

Since he didn't move, she persisted. "Now, honey..." She got up and handed him the phone.

With resignation in his voice, Red whispered, "Fine." and started dialing.

The other end of the line picked up, and a familiar voice said, "McCraith pool hall, eight ball speaking."

Red couldn't suppress a grin. "Hey Daddy."

"Tom! Great to hear from you. I'd tell your mama to pick up the other line, but she's uptown having her hair done ... *again*."

"That's okay." Red could hardly manage the words. "I was calling to see about ... maybe coming for a visit?"

Don McCraith's voice brightened. "Sure. You can stay in your grandpa's old house. Give me and your mama some time to spoil those grandkids."

"All right then," Red answered, clearing a catch in his voice. "I'll check our calendar and —"

"Tommy, what's wrong son?" His father must have heard the pain in his tone. He got right to the point. "It's your shipmates ain't it? The ones you lost."

Red swallowed hard. "I'll be okay. Really. Just takes time, right?"

A pause. "It does. But son, some things never go away. Not completely."

Against his better judgment, Red found himself slipping. "I just keep thinking. If only I'd tried... *harder*." He broke down in quiet sobs. Felt Cassie's arms wrap around him.

After a moment, his father answered gently, "It's okay, son. You're gonna get through this." Another pause, followed by a deep breath and its slow exhale. "I absolutely think you and Cassie should come for a visit. And one evening, once things settle down, you and I can talk about it over a few beers, if you want."

Red could barely respond. "Okay," he whispered. "...Sure."

Then his old man opened up in a way he never had before. "Tom. You can talk to me about anything you want, as much or as little as you need." With his next words he simultaneously cracked open a door to his past, and their future.

"You can tell me all about your friends. What a fine group of soldiers they were. How brave, stupid, and downright crazy." A sniff, followed by a short aching sigh, and then, "Hell, maybe I'll even tell you about mine."

The End

Appendix:

Detail of "The Carta Marina" - Sea Serpent

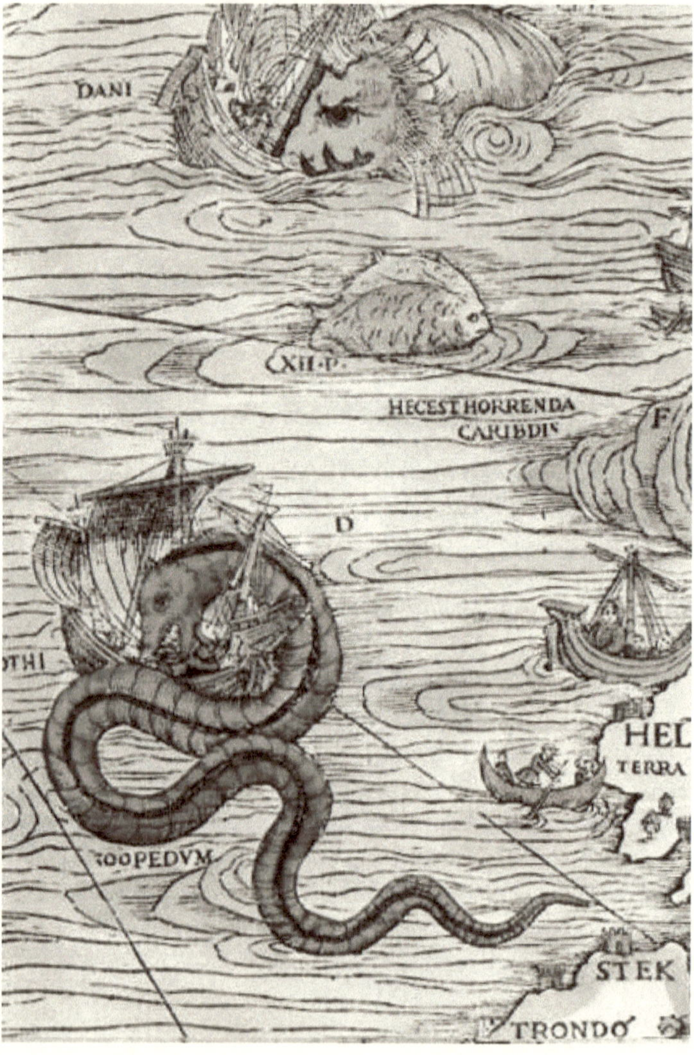

From the unclassified log entries of Intelligence Specialist Chief Thomas 'Red' McCraith

The following is a concise, yet by no means comprehensive, record of world events attributed in some part to the being known as Saxüru, whose presence in the regions surrounding the Red Sea and Persian Gulf was increasingly felt.

Eight days after Cassie and I were married, on January 17th, 1993, a guided-missile cruiser and two destroyers, steaming in the Arabian Gulf, along with a destroyer in the Red Sea, launched 42 Tomahawks on targets in Iraq. This was in response to violations of the Middle East no-fly zone.

The next month, on February 26, the World Trade Center was bombed. The intent was to topple tower 1 into tower 2 to take out both. The attempt failed but resulted in the deaths of six civilians, one of whom was seven months pregnant.

During a visit to Kuwait in April of '93, an Iraqi assassination plot was foiled, which would have killed former President George H. W. Bush, his wife, two of their sons, and former Secretary of State, James Baker.

In May 1993, trouble struck at the research facilities in Quantico. Finally realizing that his master was never coming to free him, Gurax took matters into his own hands. The JTF scientists overseeing the demi-god were unable to stop him as, right before their eyes, within the confines of his tank, he raked talons across both sides of his own throat, ripping out his gills.

On June 26, the United States responded to the assassination attempt on George H. Bush with a night attack against Iraqi intelligence in Baghdad. The guided-missile cruiser *USS Chancellorsville* launched 9 Tomahawks from the northern Arabian Gulf, while the destroyer *USS Peterson* fired 14 more from the Red Sea.

Pentagon officials stated that 16 of those missiles hit targets at which they were aimed, while 4 others landed elsewhere in the intelligence compound, and 3 struck residential housing in downtown Baghdad. President Clinton expressed regret that Iraqi civilians were killed but, on his way to church, insisted, "We sent the message we needed to send."

Through it all, Cassie and I kept tabs on things as best we could, but a few years later the first baby came. In '95 we had our precious little Abigail, named after her grandmother. Cassie made the decision to stay home and raise children. I supported that decision, furthered my career the best I could to support our growing family, and loved Cassie and my little girl with all my heart.

Still, I began to long for the sea. Just one more mission, that's all I wanted. Then maybe that saltwater call to my soul would be sated. I pushed those feelings down and pressed on, throwing myself into my family and my work. Poring over data as if the fate of the world depended on it.

Things heated up again on August 31st of '96 when an Iraqi offensive was mounted against the city of Irbil in an attempt to defuse the Kurdish Civil War. This led to Operation Desert Strike in September of that year. A guided-missile cruiser and a destroyer fired 14 Tomahawks. The next day, three destroyers and a fast attack submarine fired 17 more.

The next year, in '97, Cassie gave birth to our second child, a boy this time. We named him Hank. I never fully used my G.I. Bill. But I took classes to round out my skills and worked my way up steadily, being promoted to First Class Petty Officer and then Chief.

Another year passed. Then on August 7, 1998 Al-Qaeda launched two attacks on embassies in East Africa.

A few weeks later, on Aug. 20, the U.S. hit back as Operation Infinite Reach began with simultaneous raids. Two guided missile cruisers, two destroyers, and a fast attack submarine fired 73 Tomahawks at the Zhawar Kili al-Badr terrorist training and support complex, 30 miles southwest of Khowst, Afghanistan. Meanwhile the destroyers *USS Briscoe* and *USS Hayler*, steaming in the Red Sea, launched six Tomahawks against the al-Shifa pharmaceutical plant near Khartoum, Sudan.

The U.S. finished out 1998 with Operation Desert Fox, a four-day bombing of Iraqi targets from December 16 to 19. This was for Iraq's failure to comply with United Nations Security Council resolutions and its interference with Special Commission inspectors.

Finally, on October 12, 2000, the *USS Cole* was attacked in Yemen. I told Cassie I had to go. It was time to take out that demon once and for all.

USS Scorpius Basic Schematic and General Characteristics of *Pegasus* Class Hydrofoils

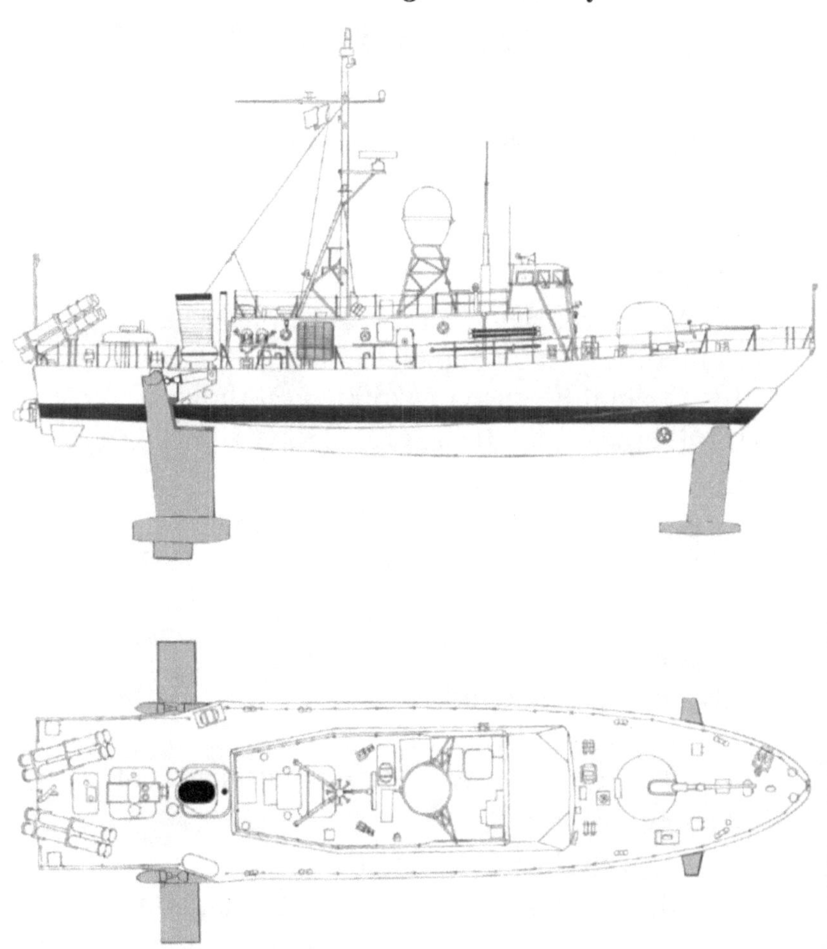

General characteristics of the Pegasus Class Hydrofoils (PHM)

Displacement: 237.2 long tons (241 t)

Length: 133 ft (41 m)

Beam: 28 ft (8.5 m)

Propulsion:
2 × Mercedes-Benz MTU marine diesels
(hullborne), 1,600 bhp (1,193 kW)
1 × General Electric LM2500 gas turbine
(Foilborne), 18,000 shp (13,423 kW)

Speed:
12 knots (22 km/h; 14 mph) hullborne
48 knots (89 km/h; 55 mph) foilborne

Complement: 4 officers, 17 enlisted

Sensors and processing systems:
LN-66 navigation radar
MK 94 Mod 1 (PHM-1),
MK 92 Mod 1 (PHM 2-6) fire-control system

Armament:
2 × quad RGM-84 Harpoon
1 × Mk 75 76 mm OTO Melara, 62 cal. gun

About the author

John S. Worth has been writing and illustrating stories since he was old enough to trace comic books. He grew up in rural Georgia reading every Tarzan novel he could get his hands on, then moved on to Asimov, Tolkien, Orson Scott Card ... you get the picture.

Since those days (way back in the twentieth century), he's served in the U.S. Navy (14 countries and about every island in the Caribbean), spent about a year undercover as a High School Science Teacher, then a Chemist for Merck Pharmaceuticals, and (according to certain sources) he's now at a Nuclear Power Plant.

What's known for sure is that he's happily married, somewhere back in Georgia, with two awesome sons. He still likes to draw and make up stories, and is really just happy and surprised to still be alive. Most of his fiction is self-published, under his own imprint, and can be found on his website, FictionWorthReading.com.

Sea Serpent is his first venture into Military-Fantasy-Adventure, and his first novel published by the excellent team at Three Ravens Publishing.